Susan Warner

The House in Town

Susan Warner

The House in Town

ISBN/EAN: 9783744649902

Printed in Europe, USA, Canada, Australia, Japan

Cover: Foto ©Andreas Hilbeck / pixelio.de

More available books at **www.hansebooks.com**

THE

HOUSE IN TOWN.

A Sequel to "Opportunities."

BY

THE AUTHOR OF

"THE WIDE WIDE WORLD."

"No man that warreth entangleth himself with the affairs of this life; that he may please him who hath chosen him to be a soldier."— 2 TIM. ii. 4.

NEW YORK:

ROBERT CARTER AND BROTHERS,

530 BROADWAY.

1872.

THE HOUSE IN TOWN.

CHAPTER I.

"OH Norton! Oh Norton! do you know what has happened?"

Matilda had left the study and rushed out into the dining-room to tell her news, if indeed it were news to Norton. She had heard his step. Norton seemed in a pre-occupied state of mind.

"Yes!" he said. "I know that confounded shoemaker has left something in the heel of my boot which is killing me."

Matilda was not like some children. She could wait; and she waited, while Norton pulled off his boot, made examinations into the interior, and went stoutly to work with penknife and file. In the midst of it he looked up, and asked, —

" What has happened to *you*, Pink ? "

" Then don't you know yet, Norton ? "

" Of course not. I would fine all shoe-makers who leave their work in such a slovenly state ! If I didn't limp all the way from the bridge here, it was because I wouldn't, — not because I wouldn't like to."

" Why not limp, if it saved your foot ? " inquired Matilda.

" *You* would, Pink, wouldn't you ? "

" Why, yes ; certainly I would."

" Well, you might," said Norton. " But did you ever read the story of the Spartan boy and the fox ? "

" No."

" He stole a fox," said Norton, working away at the inside of his boot, which gave him some trouble.

" But you haven't stolen a fox."

" I should think not," said Norton. " The boy carried the fox home under his cloak ;

and it was not a tame fox, Pink, by any means, and did not like being carried, I suppose; and it cut and bit and tore at the boy all the while, under his cloak; so that by the time he got the fox home, it had made an end of him."

" Why didn't he let the fox go?"

" Ah! why didn't he?" said Norton. " He was a boy, and he would have been ashamed."

" And you would have been ashamed to limp in the street, Norton?"

" For a nail in my boot. What is a man good for, that can't stand anything?"

" I should not have been ashamed at all."

" You're a girl," said Norton approvingly. " It is a different thing. What is your news, Pink?"

" But Norton, I don't see why it is a different thing. Why should not a woman be as brave as a man, and as strong, — in one way?"

" I suppose, because she is not as strong in

the other way.   She hasn't got it to do, Pink,
that's all.   But a man, or a boy, that can't
bear anything without limping, is a muff;
that's the whole of it."

" A muff's a nice thing," said Matilda
laughing.

" Not if it's a boy," said Norton.   " Go on
with your news, Pink.   What is it ? "

" I wonder if you know.   Oh Norton, *do*
you know what your mother and Mr. Richmond have been talking about ? "

" I wasn't there," said Norton.   " If you
were, you may tell me."

" I was not there.   But Mr. Richmond has
been talking to me about it.   Norton," — and
Matilda's voice sank, — " do you know, they
have been arranging, and your mother wishes
it, that I should *stay* with her ? "

Matilda spoke the last words very softly, in
the manner of one who makes a communica-
tion of somewhat awful character; and in
truth it had a kind of awe for her.   Evidently
not for Norton.   He had almost finished his

boot, and he kept on with his filing, as coolly as if what Matilda said had no particular interest or novelty. She would have been disappointed, but that she had caught one gleam from Norton's eye which flashed like an electric spark. She just caught it, and then Norton went on calmly, —

" I think that is a very sensible arrangement, Pink. I must say, it is not the first time it has occurred to me."

" Then you knew it before? "

" I did not know they had settled it," said Norton, still coolly.

" But you knew it was talked about? O Norton! why didn't you tell me? "

Norton looked up, smiled, dropped his boot, and at once took his new little sister in his arms and clasped her right heartily.

" What for should I tell you, Pink? " he said, kissing Matilda's eyes, where the tears of that incipient disappointment had gathered.

" How could you *help* telling me? "

" Ah, that is another thing," said Norton. " *You* couldn't have helped it, could you ? "

" But it is true now, Norton."

" Ay, it is true; and you belong to mamma and me now, Pink; and to nobody else in the wide world.   Isn't that jolly?"

" And to Mr. Richmond," Matilda added.

" Not a bit to Mr. Richmond; not a fraction," said Norton.   "He may be your guardian and your minister if you like ; and I like him too; he's a brick; but you belong to nobody in the whole world but mamma and me."

" Well, Norton," said Matilda, with a sigh of pleasure — " I'm glad."

" Glad!" said Norton.   " Now come, — let us sit right down and see some of the things we'll do."

" Yes.   But no, Norton; I must get Mr. Richmond's supper.   I shall not have many times more to do that; Miss Redwood will be soon home, you know."

" And we too, I hope.   I declare, Pink, I

believe you like getting supper. Here goes! What is to do?"

"Nothing, for you, Norton."

"Kettle on?"

"On ages ago. You may see if it is boiling."

"How can an iron kettle boil? If you'll tell me that."

"Why, the water boils that is in it. The kettle is put for the water."

"And what right have you to put the kettle for the water? At that rate, one might do all sorts of things — Now Pink, how can I tell if the water boils? The steam is coming out of the nose."

"*That's* no sign, Norton. Does it sing?"

"Sing!" said Norton. "I never learned kettle music. No, I don't think it does. It bubbles; the water in it I mean."

Matilda came in laughing. "No," she said, "it has stopped singing; and now it boils. The steam is coming out from under the cover. *That's* a sign. Now, Norton, if you like, you may make a nice plate of toast, and I'll butter it. Mr. Richmond likes toast, and he is tired to-night, I know."

" I can't make a plate," said Norton; " but I'll try for the toast. Is it good for people that are tired ? "

" Anything comfortable is, Norton."

" I wouldn't be a minister ! " said Norton softly, as he carefully turned and toasted the bread, — " I would not be a minister, for as much as you could give me."

" Why, Norton ? I think I would — if I was a man."

" He has no comfort of his life," said Norton. " This sort of a minister doesn't have. He is always going, going; and running to see people that want him, and stupid people too; he has to talk to them, all the same as if they were clever, and put up with them ; and he's always working at his sermons and getting broken off. What comfort of his life does Mr. Richmond have now ? except when you and I make toast for him ? "

"O Norton, I think he has a great deal."

"I don't see it."

Matilda stood wondering, and then smiled; the comfort of *her* life was so much just then. The slices of toast were getting brown and buttered, and made a savory smell all through the kitchen; and now Matilda made the tea, and the flowery fragrance of that added another item to what seemed the great stock of pleasure that afternoon. As Miss Redwood had once said, the minister knew a cup of good tea when he saw it; and it was one of the few luxuries he ever took pains to secure; and the sweetness of it now in the little parsonage kitchen was something very delicious. Then Matilda went and put her head in at the study door.

"Tea is ready, Mr. Richmond."

But the minister did not immediately obey the summons, and the two children stood behind their respective chairs, waiting. Matilda's face was towards the western windows.

" Are you very miserable, Pink ? " said Norton, watching her.

" I am so happy, Norton ! "

" I want to get home now," said Norton, drumming upon his chair. " I want you there. You belong to mamma and me, and to nobody else in the whole world, Pink ; do you know that ? "

Except Mr. Richmond — was again in Matilda's thoughts ; but she did not say it this time. It was nothing against Norton's claim.

" Where *is* the minister ? " Norton went on. " You called him."

" O he has got some stupid body with him, keeping him from tea."

" That is what I said," Norton repeated. " I wouldn't live such a life — not for money."

Mr. Richmond came however at this moment, looking not at all miserable; glanced at the two happy faces with a bright eye ; then for an instant they were still, while the sweet willing words of prayer went up from lips and heart to bless the board.

" What is it that you would not do for money, Norton ? " Mr. Richmond asked as he received his cup of tea.

Norton hesitated and coloured. Matilda spoke for him.

" Mr. Richmond, may we ask you something ? "

" Certainly ! " said the minister, with a quick look at the two faces.

" If you wouldn't think it wrong for us to ask. — Is the — I mean, do you think, — the life of a minister is a very hard one ? "

" So that is the question, is it ? " said Mr. Richmond smiling. " Is Norton thinking of taking the situation ? "

" Norton thinks it cannot be a comfortable life, Mr. Richmond; and I thought he was mistaken."

" What do you suppose a minister's business is, Norton ? that is the first consideration. You must know what a man has to do, before you can judge whether it is hard to do it."

" I thought I knew, sir."

" Yes, I suppose so; but it don't follow that you do."

" I know part," said Norton. " A minister has to preach sermons, and marry people, and baptize children, and read prayers at funerals and — "

" Go on," said Mr. Richmond.

" I was going to say, it seems to me, he has to talk to everybody that wants to talk to him."

" How do *you* get along with that difficulty ? " said Mr. Richmond. " It attacks other people besides ministers."

" I dodge them," said Norton. " But a minister cannot, — can he, sir? "

Mr. Richmond laughed.

" Well, Norton," he said, " you have given a somewhat sketchy outline of a minister's life; but my question remains yet, — what is the business of his life. You would not say that planing and sawing are the business of a carpenter's life — would you? "

" No, sir."

" What then ? "

" Building houses, and ships, and barns, and bridges."

" And a tailor's life is not cutting and snipping, but making clothes. So my commission is not to make · sermons. What is it ? "

Norton looked at a loss, and expectant; Matilda enjoying.

" The same that was given to the apostle Paul, and no worse. I am sent to people ' to open their eyes, and to turn them from darkness to light, and from the power of Satan to God, that they may receive forgiveness of sins, and inheritance among them which are sanctified.' "

" But I do not understand, Mr. Richmond," said Norton, after a little pause.

" What ? "

" If you will excuse me. I do not understand that. Can you open people's eyes ? "

" He who sends me does that, by means of

2

the message which I carry. ' How can they believe on him of whom they have not heard ? ' "

" I see — " said Norton very respectfully.

" You see, I am the King's messenger. And my business is, to carry the King's message. It is possible to make sermons, and not do that."

" I don't think I ever heard the message, or anything that sounded like a message, in our church," said Norton.

" Do you know what the message is ? "

Norton looked up from his toast and seemed a little taken aback.

" You might have heard it without knowing it."

" Might I ?   What is the message, sir ? "

" This is it.   That God wants and calls for the love of every human heart ; and that on his part he loves us so well, as to give his own Son to die for us, that we might be saved through him."

" Why to *die* for us ? " inquired Norton.

"Because we all deserved to die, and he took our place. 'He tasted death for every man.' So for you and for me. What do we owe to one who gave his life to ransom ours?"

"I see," — said Norton again thoughtfully. "But Mr. Richmond, people do not always hear the message — do they?"

"You can tell," said Mr. Richmond, shortly.

"I see!" repeated Norton. "It isn't making sermons. I don't see, though, why it isn't a hard life."

"That requires another explanation, but it is not difficult. How would one naturally feel, Norton, towards another, who by his own suffering and death had saved him when he was bound to die?"

"You mean, who had done it on purpose?" said Norton.

"On purpose. Just because he loved the lost one."

"Why," said Norton, "if the man had any heart in him" —

" Well? What then ? "

" Why, he wouldn't think that his *hand* was his own."

" He would belong to his redeemer ? "

" Yes, sir."

" So I think, Norton.   Then, tell me, do you think it would be hard work to do anything to please or serve such a friend? Would even hardships seem hard ? "

" I can't think what *would* seem hard," said Norton eagerly.

But then a silence fell upon the little party.   Matilda had opened all her ears to hear Norton speak in this manner; she was excited; she almost thought that he was about to enter into the life he seemed to understand so well; but Mr. Richmond went on with his tea quite composedly, and Norton was a little embarrassed.   What was the matter?   Matilda wished some one would speak again; but Mr. Richmond sent his cup to be filled, and stirred it, and took another piece of toast, and Norton never raised his eyes from his plate.

" That idea is new to you, my boy ? " said Mr. Richmond at last, smiling.

" I never — well, yes; — I do not understand those things," said Norton.

" You understood *this* ? "

" Your words ; yes, sir."

" And the thing which my words meant ? "

" I suppose — yes, I suppose I do," said Norton.

" Do you understand the bearing of it on all of us three at the table."

Norton looked up inquiringly.

" You comprehend how it touches me ? "

" Yes, sir," — Norton answered with profound respect in eye and voice.

" And Matilda ? "

The boy's eye went quick and sharp to the little figure at the head of the table. What his look meant, Matilda could not tell; and he did not speak.

" You comprehend how it touches Matilda ? " Mr. Richmond repeated.

" No, sir," was answered rather stoutly. It

had very much the air of not wanting to know.

"You should understand, if you are to live in the same house together. The same Friend has done the same kindness for Matilda that he has done for me; he has given himself to death that she might live; and she has heard it and believed it, and obeyed his voice and become his servant. What sort of life ought she to live?"

Norton stared at Mr. Richmond, not in the least rudely, but like one very much discomfited. He looked as if he were puzzling to find his way out of a trap. But Matilda clapped her hands together, exclaiming,

"I am so glad Norton understands that! I never could make him understand it."

"Why you never tried," said Norton.

"O yes, I did, Norton; in different ways. I suppose I never said it so that you could understand it."

"I don't understand it now," said Norton.

" O Mr. Richmond! don't he ? " said Matilda.

" 'Tell him," said the minister. " Perhaps you put it too cautiously. Tell him in words that he cannot mistake, what sort of life you mean to lead."

The little girl hesitated and looked at Norton. Norton, like one acting under protest, looked at her. They waited, questioning each other's faces.

" It is that, Norton," Matilda said at last very gently, and with a sort of tenderness in tone and manner which spoke for her. " It is just that you said. I do not think that my *hand* is my own."

Norton looked at the little hand unconsciously extended to point her words, as if he would have liked to confiscate it; he made no reply, but turned to his supper again. The conversation had taken a turn he did not welcome.

" We have not done with the subject," Mr. Richmond went on. " You see how it touches me now, and how it touches Matilda. You know by your own shewing, what sort of life she ought to lead ; and so you will know how you ought to help her and not hinder her in it. But Norton, — how does it touch you ? "

The boy was not ready with an answer. Then he said, —

" I don't see that it touches me any way, sir."

" On honour ? " said Mr. Richmond gently. " That same Friend has done the same kindness for you."

Norton looked as if he wished it were not true ; and as if very unwilling to admit anything.

" I wish you could hear what I hear," said Mr. Richmond. " So many voices ! — "

" What, sir ? " asked both the children at once.

" So many voices ! " repeated Mr. Richmond. " I hear the voice of love now, from the skies, speaking that soft, sweet ' Come ! '

in the heart. I hear my own voice giving the message. I hear the promise to them who seek for glory, honour, and immortality. And I hear the sound of the harps of those who have a new song to sing, which none can learn but the hundred and forty and four thousand which have been redeemed from the earth. And I hear the rejoicing in heaven of those who will say, ' Thou wast slain, and hast redeemed us to God by thy blood, out of every kindred and tongue and people and nation ; and hast made us unto our God kings and priests, and we shall reign on the earth.' And then there is a throne and a judgment seat, and I hear a voice that says, ' Well done, good and faithful servant ; enter thou into the joy of thy Lord.' — "

Mr. Richmond's voice had fallen a little ; his eyes were cast down. Norton's eyes were downcast too, and his face ; it did not respond, as Matilda's face did ; and when the party rose from table a minute or two afterwards, Norton made use of his liberty to quit

the room and the house.   Matilda brought her
tub of water to wash up the cups and plates.
Mr. Richmond had gone off to his study.

The little girl touched the china with soft
delicate fingers; lifted each piece and set it
down with gentle noiselessness; the little
clink of the china keeping measure, perhaps,
with the thoughts which moved and touched,
so gently, in her heart.   Presently Mr. Richmond came out again.   He walked up and
down the little room several times; it was a
small walk, for a very few of his steps took
him from one corner to the other; then he
came and stood beside the table where
Matilda was at work.   The child stopped
and looked up at him wistfully.   Their eyes
met; and a smile of much love and confidence was exchanged between the two.

"Mr. Richmond, —" said Matilda, "isn't
it difficult, sometimes, to *keep* hearing those
voices ? "

You could see the light spring into the
young man's eyes; but he answered very
quietly, "Why, Matilda ? "

" I think it is difficult," the child repeated.

" You find it so?"

" I think, sometimes, Mr. Richmond, I don't hear them at all."

" It is not necessary to be always thinking about them."

" No, I know that; but sometimes I seem to get out of the sound of them."

" How comes that?"

" I don't know. I think it must be because I am hearing other voices so much."

" You are right." Mr. Richmond began his pacing up and down again. Matilda stood with a cup in her hands which she had been washing, the water dripping from her fingers and it into the tub.

" How can I help it, Mr. Richmond?"

Mr. Richmond was thinking perhaps of Fenelon's words: " O how rare is it, to find a soul still enough to hear God speak!" — but he did not quote them to the child. He stood still again.

" Tilly, when one gets out of hearing of

those voices, the enemy has a good chance to whisper to us; and he never loses a chance. That was what happened to Eve in the garden of Eden."

" How can I do, Mr. Richmond?"

" I should say, dear, don't get out of hearing of them."

" But, sometimes " — Matilda paused in difficulty. " Sometimes I am thinking of so many other things, and my head gets full; and then I do not know where I am."

Mr. Richmond smiled. " You could not have given a better description of the case," he said. " But Matilda, when you find that you do not know where you are, run away, shut yourself up, and find out. It isn't safe to get out of hearing of the Lord's voice."

" O Mr. Richmond! " said the child. " I want to be where I can hear it all the time."

" There is one way. Don't you know it?"

" No, sir; I don't think I do."

" My dear child, it is very simple. Only obey his voice when you hear it, and it will always be with you. Obedience is the little key that unlocks the whole mystery, — the whole mystery," said Mr. Richmond, beginning to walk up and down again. " When you hear ever so soft a whisper in your heart, saying, ' *This* is the way,' follow there; and so the Lord will lead you always."

Mr. Richmond went off to his study, but paused again to say, " Study the twenty third verse of the fourteenth chapter of John, Matilda; and take that for your rule."

Matilda went about softly, putting the china in the pantry, making the table clean, hanging up her towel and putting away her tub. Just as she had finished, Mr. Richmond opened the door. He had his hat and great coat on.

" Tilly, look after my fire, will you? " he said. " I shall be gone some time probably."

CHAPTER II.

MATILDA went to the study. It was in winter trim now. The red curtains fell over the windows; a carpet had replaced or covered the summer mat; the lamp was lighted, but burned low; and a fire of nut wood sticks blazed and crackled softly in the chimney. The whole room was sweet with the smell of it. Matilda sat down on the rug in front of the blaze; but she was hardly there when she heard the front door open and Norton come in. So she called him to the study.

"Is the dominie gone out?" said Norton, as he entered Mr. Richmond's sanctum.

"Gone out for a good while, he said. You and I have got to take care of the fire." And Matilda threw herself down on the rug again.

" This is jolly," said Norton.

" Isn't it?" said Matilda. " It is so nice here. And do you smell, Norton, how sweet it is with the hickory wood?"

" That isn't hickory," said Norton. " It's oak."

" Part of it is hickory, Norton, I know. But I suppose oak is sweet."

" I think everything is sweet to you," said Norton.

" I do think it is," said Matilda. " Everything is to-night, I am sure. Everything. Isn't this just as pleasant as it can be?"

" It's jolly," said Norton. "Let's have on another stick. Now we can think and talk what we will do."

" What we will *do*, Norton?" Matilda repeated.

" Yes. We've got no end of things to do. Why, now we can do what we like, Pink. You aren't going away any more; and we can just lay our plans in comfort."

" I did'nt know we had any plans to lay,"

said Matilda. She looked as if the present
was good enough. The firelight shone on
a little figure and face of most utter content-
ment, there down on the rug; a soft little
head, a very gentle face, but alive with pleasant thoughts.

"We want to get home now," continued
Norton.

"But it is pleasant here, too. O Norton!"
Matilda broke out suddenly, "you don't
know how pleasant! Now I can take the
good of it. I did before, in a way; but then
I was always thinking it would maybe stop
to-morrow. Now it will never stop; I am
so glad!"

"What will never stop?"

"O I don't know. It seems to me my
happiness will never stop. You don't know
anything about it, Norton. To think I am
not to go back to that old life again — I was
afraid of it every day; and now to-night
at tea, and *now*, I am as happy as I can be.
I can't think of it enough."

" Of what, Pink ? "

" Of that. That I am not to go back to aunt Candy any more."

" What do you think of where you *are* going ? " asked Norton a little jealously. But his face cleared the next instant.

" Norton," said Matilda, " I *can't* think of it, — not yet. It is too good to think of all at once. I have to take part at a time. If I did think of it, I don't know but it would seem too good to be true."

" Well it isn't," said Norton. " Now Pink, we'll fix those hyacinth and tulip beds all right. You haven't chosen your bulbs yet. And then, when we have planted our bulbs — I hope it is not too late yet, but I declare I don't know! — perhaps we'll leave the winter to take care of them, and we'll go off to New York till spring. How would you like that ? "

" I don't care where I go," said Matilda, — " with you and Mrs. Laval."

" You never saw New York, did you ? "

3

" No, never. Is it pleasanter than Briery Bank, Norton ? "

" Well, not when the tulips are out, perhaps; ·but in the cold weather it's jolly enough. It's queer, though."

" Queer ? " repeated Matilda curiously.

" I wonder if you wouldn't think so," said Norton. " I don't mean. New York, you know ; that's all right ; but our house."

" I didn't know you had a house in New York," said Matilda.

" No, of course not; how should you ? but now it's different. Pink, it is very jolly !" said Norton, quitting his seat in the chimney corner and coming down on the rug beside Matilda. " That's a good fire to roast chestnuts."

" Is it ? but we haven't any chestnuts to roast," said Matilda.

" That's another thing you don't know," said Norton. " We've got a lot of chestnuts, — splendid ones, too. I'll fetch 'em, and we'll roast some. It's the very best way."

Norton went off for a basket, which proved to be full of brown, plump chestnuts, large and shining as they should be. Sitting down upon the rug again he began to prepare some for roasting, by cutting a small bit off one corner. Matilda picked up these bits of skin and threw them into the fire as fast as they were cut.

"Never mind," said Norton. "We'll sweep 'em up in a heap at the end, and make one job of it."

"But Mr. Richmond might come in."

"Well, — he has seen chestnuts before," said Norton coolly.

"I don't believe he has seen people cutting and roasting them in his study, though."

"All right. We'll give him some."

"But what are you doing that for, Norton?"

"Did you never roast chestnuts, Pink?"

"No. We never had a fireplace, with wood, I mean, in our house."

"It's a good sort of thing to have in any

house," said Norton. " I believe I'll have
'em all through my house."

" Your house ? "

" Yes.   I shall have a house some day ;
and then you and mamma will live with me."

Matilda could not see the reason for this
inversion of arrangements, and she was
silent a little while ; studying it, without
success.

" But what *are* you cutting these little
pieces off for, Norton ? "

" Why, they'd fly if I didn't."

" What would fly ? "

" Why the chestnuts, Pink !   They would
fly all over."

" Out of the fire ? "

" Yes.   Certainly."

" What would make them fly ? and how
will that hinder it ? "

Norton sat back on the rug — he had been
bending over to screen his face from the heat
of the blaze — and looked at Matilda with very
benevolent, laughing eyes.

" Pink, the chestnuts are green."

" Aren't they ripe ? " said Matilda. " They look so."

" Yes, yes, they are ripe; but what I mean is, that they are fresh; they are not dry. There is a great deal of water in them."

" Water ? " said Matilda.

" Not standing in a pool, you know; but in the juice, or sap, or whatever you call it. Well, you know that fire makes water boil?"

" Yes."

" And when water turns into steam, you know it takes room ? "

" Yes, I know," said Matilda.

" Well, that's it. When steam begins to make in the chestnut, the skin won't hold it; and unless I cut a place for it to get out, it will burst the chestnut. And when it bursts, the chestnuts will generally jump."

" Yes, I understand," said Matilda.

" And wherever it jumps to, it will be apt to make a hole in the carpet."

" But, Norton! I should think if the steam

made very fast, in a hot place, you know, it might burst the chestnut in spite of the hole you have cut."·

"Ay," said Norton. "That does happen occasionally. We'll be on the look-out."

Then he prepared a nice bed of ashes, laid the chestnuts in carefully, and covered them up artistically, first with ashes and then with coals. Matilda watched the process with great interest, and a little wonder what Mr. Richmond would think of it. However, he had said that he was likely to be out for some time, and it was now only half past seven o'clock. The fire burned gently, and the ash-bed of chestnuts looked very promising.

"What was it you said was jolly, when you came and sat down on the rug here, Norton?"

"I don't know."

"You said, ' Pink, it is very jolly ! ' "

"The fire, I guess. O, I know!" said Norton. "I meant *this*, Pink; that it is very

capital we have got you now, and you belong to us, and whatever we do, we shall do
together. I was thinking of that, I know,
and of the New York house. Hallo!"

For an uneasy chestnut at this instant
made a commotion in the bed of ashes; and
presently another leaped clean out. But it
was not roasted enough, Norton affirmed,
and so was put back.

" What about the New York house?" said
Matilda then.

" Why, a good many things, you'll find,"
said Norton; " and people too. You've got
to know about it now. It's my grandmother's house, to begin with. Look out!
there's another chestnut."

Matilda wondered that she had never heard
of this lady before; though she did not say so.

" It is my grandmother's house," Norton
repeated, as he recovered the erring chestnut;
" and *she* would like that we should be there
always; but there is more to be said about
it. I have an aunt living there; an aunt

that married a Jew; her husband is dead, and now she makes her home with my grandmother; she and her two children, my cousins."

"Then you have cousins!" Matilda repeated.

"Two Jew cousins. Yes."

"Are *they* Jews?"

"*She* isn't, my aunt isn't; but they are. Judith is a real little Jewess, with eyes as black as a dewberry, and as bright; and David — well, *he's* a Jew."

"How old are they?"

"About as old as we are. There's a chestnut, Pink! it went over there."

That chestnut was captured, and kept and eaten; and Matilda said she had never eaten anything so good in the shape of a chestnut.

"Of course you haven't," said Norton. "That one wasn't done, though. We must leave them a little while longer."

"And when you're in the city you all live together?" Matilda went on.

" When we are in the city we all live together. And grandmamma never will leave
aunt Judy, and aunt Judy never will come
up here; so in the summer we *don't* all live
together. And I am glad of it."

Matilda wanted very much to ask why,
but she did not. Norton presently went
on.

" It is all very well in the winter. But
then I am going to school all the while, and
there isn't so much time for things. And I
like driving here better than in the park."

" What is the park ? " Matilda inquired.

" You don't know ! " exclaimed Norton.
" That's good fun. Promise me, Pink, that
you will go with nobody but me the first
time. Promise me ! "

" Why, whom should I go with, Norton ?
Who would take me ? "

" I don't know. Mamma might, or grandmother might, or aunt Judy. Promise,
Pink."

" Well, I will not, if I can help it," said

Matilda. " But how funny it is that I should be making you such a promise."

" Ay, isn't it?" said Norton. " There will be a good many such funny things, you'll find."

" But how are these cousins of yours Jews, Norton, when their mother is not a Jew ? "

" Jewess," said Norton. " Why, because their father *was*, — a Jew, I mean. He was a Spanish Jew; and my aunt and cousins have lived in Spain till three years ago. How should a boy with his name, David Bartholomew, be anything but a Jew ? "

" Bartholomew is English, isn't it ? "

" Yes, the name. O they are not Spaniards entirely; only the family has lived out there for ever so long. They have relations enough in New York. I wish they hadn't."

" But how are they Jews, Norton ? Don't they believe — what we believe ? " Matilda's voice sunk.

" What we believe ? " repeated Norton. " Part of it, I suppose. They are not like

Hindoos or Chinese. But you had better not talk to them just as you talked to Mr. Richmond to-night."

"But, Norton — I must live so."

"Live how you like; *they* have got nothing to do with your living. Now, Pink, I think we'll overhaul those chestnuts, — if you've no objection."

It was very exciting, getting the roasted fruit out from among the ashes and coals, burning their fingers, counting the chestnuts, and eating them; and then Norton prepared a second batch, that they might, as he said, have some to give to Mr. Richmond. Eating and cooking, a great deal of talk went on all the while. Eight o'clock came, and nine; and still not Mr. Richmond. Norton went out to look at the weather, as far as the piazza steps; and came in powdered with snow. It was thickly falling, he said; so the two children went to work again. It was impossible to sit there with the chestnuts and not eat them; so Norton roasted a third quantity. Just as these were reclaimed from the ashes, Mr. Richmond came in. He looked tired.

"So you have kept my hearth warm for me," he said; "and provided me supper. Thank you."

"We have done no harm, sir, I hope," said Norton; "though it was in your study."

"My study was the very place," said Mr. Richmond. "You cannot get such a fire everywhere; and my fire does not often have such pleasant use made of it. I shall miss you both."

"How soon shall we be ordered away, sir?" Norton asked.

"Your mother said to-morrow; but at the rate the snow is falling, that will hardly be. It looks like a great storm, or feels like it rather. It's impossible to *see*."

A great storm it proved the next morning. The snow was falling very thick; it lay heaped on the branches of the pines, and drifted into a great bank at the corner of the piazza, and blocked up the window-sills. It was piled up high on the house steps, and had quite covered all signs of path and roadway; the little sweep in front of the house was levelled and hid; the track to the barn could not be traced any longer. And still the snow came down, in gentle, swift, stayless supply; fast piling up fresh beautiful feathers of crystal on those that already settled soft upon all the earth. So Matilda found things when she got up in the morning. The air was dark with the snow-clouds, and yet light with a beautiful light from the universal whiteness; and the air was sweet with the pure sweetness of the falling snow. Matilda hurried down. It was Sunday morning.

" There'll be no getting away to-day," said Norton, as together they set the breakfast in readiness.

" Miss Redwood can't come home either," said Matilda. She was privately glad. A snowy Sunday at the parsonage, one more Sunday, would be pleasant.

" You can't get to church either," Norton went on.

" Why Norton! This little bit of way? It isn't but half a dozen steps."

" It is several half dozen," said Norton; " and the snow is all of a foot deep, and in places it has drifted, and there isn't a sign of anybody coming to clear it away yet. I don't believe there'll be twenty people in church, anyhow. It's falling as thick as it can."

" Mr. Ulshoeffer will clear it away in front of the church," said Matilda. " Some people will come. There! there's somebody at our back steps now."

Norton opened the kitchen door to see if it was true; and to his great astonishment found Mr. Richmond, in company with a large wooden shovel, clearing the snow from the steps and kitchen area.

" Good morning!" said the minister, from out of the snow.

" Good morning, sir. Mr. Richmond! isn't

there somebody coming to do that for you, sir ? "

" I don't know who is to come," said the minister pleasantly. " You had better shut the door and keep warm."

" Tell him breakfast is ready, Norton," Matilda cried.

" Well!" said Norton, shutting the door and coming in. " Do you mean to say that Mr. Richmond shovels his own snow ? "

" His own snow!" repeated Matilda, with a little burst of laughter. " Which part of the snow is Mr. Richmond's ? "

" What lies on his own ground, I should say. Why don't he have some one come to do it ? "

" I don't know," said Matilda ; and she looked grave now. " I don't know who there is to come to do it."

" There are people enough to do anything for money," said Norton. " Don't he have somebody come to do it ? "

" I don't know," said Matilda. " If he

had, I do not think he would do it himself."

" Then he gets very shabby treatment," said
Norton ; " that's all. I tell you, shovelling
snow is work ; and cold work at that."

" I suppose the people can't give great
pay to their minister," said Matilda.

" Then they can come and clear away the
snow for him. They have hands enough, if
they haven't the cash. I wonder if they let
him do it for himself always ? "

" I don't know."

" Well, if I was a minister," said Norton,
" which I am glad I'm not, I'd have a church
where people could give me enough pay to
keep my hands out of the snow ! "

" Hush ! " said Matilda. " Breakfast is
ready, and Mr. Richmond is coming in."

The little dining-room was more pleasant
than ever that morning. The white brightness that came in through the snowy air
seemed to make fire and warmth and breakfast particularly cosy. And there was a

hush, and a purity, and a crisp frost in the air, filling that Sunday morning with especial delights. But Mr. Richmond eat his breakfast like a man who had business on hand.

"Norton thinks there will not be many people at church, Mr. Richmond."

"There will be one," said Mr. Richmond. "And that he may get there, I have a good deal of work yet to do."

"More snow, sir?" inquired Norton.

"All the way from here to the church porch."

"Won't somebody come to do it, sir, and save you the trouble?"

"I can't tell," said the minister laughing. "Nobody ever did yet."

Norton said nothing; but Matilda was very much pleased that after breakfast he took a spade and joined Mr. Richmond in his work. Matilda never forgot that day. The snow continued to fall; flickering irregularly through the pine leaves and leaving a goodly portion of its stores gathered on the branches

4

and massing on the tufts of foliage. Else-
where the fall of the white flakes was steady
and thick as the advance of an army of
soldiers. No other resemblance between the
two things. This was all whiteness and
peace and hush and shelter for earth's needs.
Matilda stood at the study window and
watched it come down; watched the two
dark figures working away in the deep snow
to clear the path; watched to see the shovel-
fuls of snow flung right and left with a will,
and then to see the workers stop to take
breath, and lean upon their shovels and talk.
Norton was getting to know Mr. Richmond;
Matilda was glad of that. Then Mr. Ulshoeffer rang the old church bell, and she went
to make herself ready for church.

The storm continued, and there were few
people out, as Norton had said. In the afternoon the Sunday school had a very small
number, and the service did not last long.
And then Matilda sat in the hush, at the
study window, for Mr. Richmond had been

called out; and thought of the change that had fallen on her life. The path to the church was getting covered up again even already. Suddenly some one came behind her and laid hands on her shoulders, and Norton's voice demanded what she was doing?

" I was only looking, — and thinking."

" You're always at one or the other," said Norton, giving the shoulders a little shake. " *Both* is too much at once."

" O Norton, how can one help it? It's so grand, to think that God is so rich and great, and can do such beautiful things."

" What now?" said Norton.

" What now? Why, the snow."

" Oh!" said Norton. " I've seen snow before."

" But it's always just so beautiful. No, not always, for it's a grand storm to-day. Just see how it comes down. It is getting dusk already. And every flake of it is just so lovely and wonderful. Mr. Richmond shewed me some on his hat once. I am so glad to know that God made it, and there is no end to the beautiful things he can make. It's covering your walk up again, Norton."

" It's very queer to hear you talk," said Norton.

" Queer?" said Matilda.

" It's so queer, that you have no idea, Pink, how queer it is. I don't know what you want."

"I know what I want," said Matilda. "I want to know more of God's beautiful work. Mr. Richmond says the earth is full of it; and I think it would be nice to be seeing it always; but I know so little."

" You'll learn," said Norton. "I wonder if mamma will send you to school, Pink? We must get home to-morrow! We have staid a terrible long time at the parsonage."

CHAPTER III.

WHEN Matilda came down stairs the next morning to get breakfast, she found Miss Redwood in the kitchen. The fire was going, the kitchen was warm; Miss Redwood was preparing some potatoes for baking.

"Good morning!" said she. "Here I am again. It does seem funny to be washing the potatoes to put in the stove, just as if folks hadn't been sick and dying, you may say, and getting well, and all that, since I touched 'em last. Well! life's a queer thing; and it don't go by the rule of three, not by no means."

"What rule does it go by?" said Matilda, leaning on the table and looking up at the housekeeper.

" La! I don't know," said Miss Redwood. " I know what I've been workin' by all these weeks, pretty much; I kept at my multiplication table; but I couldn't get no further most days than the very beginning — ' Once one is one.' I tried hard to make it out two; but 'twas beyond me. I've learned that much, anyhow."

" Didn't Mrs. Laval help ? "

" She helped all she could, poor critter, till she was 'most beat out. I declare I was sorry for her, next to the sick ones. She did all she could. She turned in to cook; and she didn't know no more about it than I know about talkin' any language beside my own. Not so much; for I kin tell French when I hear it; but she didn't know boiling water."

" What can I do to help you, Miss Redwood ? " Matilda asked, suddenly remembering the present.

" There aint nothin' to do, child, 'cept what I'm doin'. The breakfast table is sot. I guess you've had *your* hands full, as well as the rest of us. But I declare you've kept things pretty straight. I don't let the butter set in the pantry, though ; it goes down cellar when I'm to home."

" That kitchen pantry is cold, Miss Redwood."

" It's too cold, child. Butter hadn't ought to be where it kin freeze, or get freezing hard ; it takes the sweetness out of it. You didn't know that. And the broom and pan I left at the head of the coal stairs. They ain't there now."

Matilda fetched them.

" The minister said you kept things in train, as if you'd been older," Miss Redwood went on. " I was always askin' ; and he made me feel pretty comfortable. He said *he* was."

" We have had a very nice time, Miss Redwood. We hadn't the least trouble about anything."

" Trouble was our meat and drink down yonder," said Miss Redwood. " I thought

two o' them poor furriners would surely give
up; but they didn't; and it's over with.
Praise the Lord! And I'm as glad to be
home again as if I had found a fortin. But
I was glad to be there, too. When a man —
or a woman — knows she's in her place, she's
just in the pleasantest spot she kin get to ; so
I think. And I knew I was in my place
there. But dear, Mrs. Laval thinks your
place is with her now ; so she bid me tell you
to be ready."

" When ? "

" Well, some time along in the morning
she will send the carriage to bring you, she
said."

" Has Francis come back ? "

" Who's Francis ? "

" I mean the coachman."

" I don't know nobody's names," said Miss
Redwood; " 'cept the men I took care of;
and I guess I had my own names for them.
I couldn't pucker my mouth to call them after
Mrs. Laval."

" Why, what did you call them?" said
Matilda. " I know what their names were;
they were Jules and Pierre Failly. What did
you call them?"

" It didn't make no odds," said Miss Redwood, " so long as they knew I was speaking
to 'em; and *that* they knew; 'cause when I
raised one man's head up, he knew I warn't
speaking to the other man. I called one of
'em Johnson, and 'tother Peter. It did just
as well. I dare say now," said Miss Redwood,
with a bit of a smile on her face, " they
thought Johnson meant beef tea, and Peter
meant a spoonful of medicine. It did just as
well. Come, dear; you may go get the
coffee canister for me; for now I'm in a
hurry. There ain't coffee burned for breakfast."

It was Matilda's last breakfast at the parsonage. . She could have been sorry, only
that she was so glad. After breakfast she
had her bag to pack; and a little later the
grey ponies trotted round the sweep and drew

up at the door. Matilda had watched them
turning in at the gate and coming down the
lane, stepping so gayly to the sound of their
bells; and they drew a dainty light sleigh
covered with a wealth of fine buffalo robes.
The children bade good bye to Mr. Richmond, and jumped in, and tucked the buffalo robes round them; the ponies shook
their heads and began to walk round the
sweep again; then getting into the straight
line of the lane, away they went with a merry
pace, making the snow fly.

It seemed to Matilda that such a feeling
of luxury had never come over her as she felt
then. The sleigh was so easy; the seats
were so roomy; the buffalo robes were so soft
and warm and elegant, and she was so happy.
Norton pulled one of the robes up so as
almost to cover her; no cold could get at her,
for her feet were in another. Furs over and
under her, she had nothing to do but to look
and be whirled along over the smooth snow
to the tune of the sleigh bells. It was charm-

ing, to look and see what the snow had done with the world. Thick, thick mantles of it lay upon the house roofs; how could it all stay there? The trees were loaded, bending their heads and drooping their branches under the weight which was almost too much for them. The fences had a pretty dressing, like the thick white frosting of a cake; the fields and gardens and roadway lay hidden under the soft warm carpet that was spread everywhere. But the snow clouds were all gone; and the clearest bright blue sky looked down through the white-laden tree branches.

" How much there is of it!" said Matilda.

" What?" said Norton.

" Why, I mean snow, Norton."

" Oh! Yes; there is apt to be a good deal of it," said Norton, " when it falls as hard as it can all one day and two nights."

" But Norton, to think that all that snow is just those elegant little star feathers piled up; all over the fields and house roofs, a foot and a half thick, it is all those feathery stars!"

" Well," said Norton; " what of it ? "

" Why it is wonderful," said Matilda. " It almost seems like a waste, doesn't it ? only that couldn't be."

" A waste ? " said Norton. " A waste of what ? "

" Why nobody sees, or thinks, that the street is covered with such beautiful things — the street and the fields and the houses; people only think it is snow, and that's all; when it is just little wonders of beauty, of a great many sorts too. It seems very strange."

" Only to you," said Norton. " It'll be rich to shew you things."

" But why do you suppose it is so, Norton ? I should like to ask Mr. Richmond."

" Mr. Richmond couldn't tell," said Norton.

" It must be that God is so rich," Matilda went on reverently. " So rich ! " she repeated, looking at the piled-up burden of snow along the house roofs of the street. " But then,

Norton, he must care to have things beautiful."

" Pink !" exclaimed Norton, looking at his little companion with an air half of amusement and half of something like vexation.

" Well, don't you think so ? Because nobody sees those white feathers of frost piled up there, and these that the horses are treading under feet. They do nobody any good."

" It does you good to know they are there," said Norton.

" That's true !" exclaimed Matilda. " O I'm very glad to know about them ; and I am very glad the snow is so wonderful; and I am glad to feel that God is so rich, and that he has made things so beautiful."

There was something in this speech that jarred upon Norton ; something, though he could not have told what it was, that seemed to separate Matilda from him ; there was a sweet, innocent kind of *appropriation* which he could not share; it told of relations in

which Matilda stood and to which he was
a stranger. Norton liked nothing that seemed
like division between them; but he did not
find anything just then to say, and remained
silent; while Matilda rode along in a kind
of glorious vision that was half heavenly and
half earthly. That was this snowy morning
to her. Covered up warm in the furs of the
sleigh, she leaned back and used her eyes;
rejoicing in the white brilliance of the earth
and the sunny blue of the heaven, and finding strange food for joy in them; or what
appears strange to those who do not know it.
The sleigh rushed along, past houses and
shops and the familiar signs hung out along
the street; then reaching the corner, whirled
round to the left. Matilda's home, until now,
had always lain the other way. She turned
her head and looked back, up the street.

"What is it?" Norton asked.

"Nothing — except that I am so glad not
to be going that way."

"No," said Norton. "Not that way any
more. We have got you, Pink."

"I don't understand it," said Matilda. "It makes me dizzy when I think of it."

"Here we are!" cried Norton, as the horses wheeled in through the iron gate. "It's all snow, Pink; it will be too late to plant our tulips and hyacinths."

But even that was forgotten, as the sleigh stopped, and Norton helped Matilda out from under the furs, and she realized that she had come home. Home; yes, when her feet stepped upon the marble pavement of the hall she said to herself that this was *home.* It was very strange. But Mrs. Laval's warm arms were not strange; they were easy to understand; she would hardly let Matilda out of them, and kissed her and kissed her. The kisses were instead of words; *they* said that Matilda had come home.

"Run up now, dear, to your room," she said at last, "and get your wraps off. I have somebody here to see me on business; but I will come to you by and by."

Dismissed with more kisses, Matilda went

up the stairs like one in a dream. Sharp and
snowy as the world was without, here, inside
the hall door, it was an atmosphere of summer. Soft warm air was around her as she
mounted the stairs; in Mrs. Laval's room a
wood fire was burning; in her own, oh joy!
there was a little coal fire in the grate; all
bright and blazing. Matilda slowly drew off
her things and looked around her. The pretty
green furniture with the rosebuds painted
on it, this was her own now; a warm carpet covered the mat; the bed with its luxurious belongings was something she had not
now to say good bye to; the time of parting
had not come after all; would never come,
as long as she lived. Slowly Matilda pulled
off hood and gloves and moccasins, and went
to the window. It was her own window!
The hills and the country in view from it were
hers to look at whenever she pleased. Mrs.
Candy's bell could not sound there to break
in upon anything. The child was so happy
that she was almost afraid; it seemed too

good to be really true and lasting. Gradually, as she stood there by the window, looking at what seemed to her "the treasures of
the snow," it came to her mind what she had
been thinking about that; the myriads of
wonderfully fashioned, exquisite crystal stars,
for every one of which God took care. Then
she remembered, "the hairs of your head are
all numbered;" and if so, of course no event
that happened to any of God's children could
be without meaning or carelessly sent. And
also, if he was so rich in the beauty and per-
fectness of the snow supply for the earth, he
was rich toward his children too, and would
and could give them what were the best
things for them. But then came the question; if he had brought a child like her into
these new circumstances, into such a new
home, what did he mean her to do with it?
what use should she make of it? what effect
was it intended to have upon her and upon
her life? This seemed a very great question
to Matilda. She softly shut her door and

took out her Bible and kneeled down beside it. She would study and pray till she found out.

' It happened well that Mrs. Laval's man of business kept her a good while. All that while Matilda kept up her study and search. Nevertheless she was puzzled. It was a question too large for her. All she could make out amounted to this; that she must be careful not to forget whose child she was; that before Mrs. Laval she owed love and obedience to her Saviour; that she must be on the watch for opportunities; and not allow her new circumstances to distract or divert her from them or make her unfitted for them when they came.

"I think I must watch," was Matilda's conclusion. "I might forget. Norton will want me to do things, — and Mrs. Laval will want me to do other things, — perhaps other people yet. If I keep to Mr. Richmond's rule — ' Whether ye eat or drink, or whatsoever ye do, do all to the Lord Jesus,' — I shall be sure to be right; and He will teach me."

Some very earnest prayer ended in this conclusion. Then the question came up in Matilda's mind, what opportunities were likely to spring out of her new, changed circumstances? She could not tell; she found she could do nothing with that question; she could only leave it, and watch, and wait.

She opened her door then, to be ready for Mrs. Laval's coming; and presently the soft step and gentle rustle of drapery reminded Matilda anew that she had done for ever with Mrs. Candy's plump footfall and buckram skirts.

"My darling," said Mrs. Laval, "you have been all this time alone!" She took Matilda in her arms and sat down with her, looking at her as one examines a new, precious possession.

"You smile, as if being alone was nothing very dreadful," she went on.

"I don't think it is," said Matilda.

"I do! But you and I will not be alone any more, darling, will we? Norton is a boy; he must go and come; but you are my own — my little daughter! — yes, now and always."

She clasped Matilda in her arms and kissed her with lips that trembled very much; trembled so much that Matilda was afraid she would break into a passion of tears again; but that was restrained. After a little she sat back, and stroking Matilda's hair from her brow, asked softly, —

"And what do *you* say to it, Matilda?"

Matilda tried to find words and could not; trembled; was very near crying for her own part; finally answered in the only way. In her turn she threw her arms round Mrs. Laval's neck; in her turn kissed cheeks and lips, giving herself up for the first time to the feeling of the new relationship between them. The lady did not let her go, but sat still with her arms locked around Matilda and Matilda's head in her neck and both of them motionless, for a good while.

" Will you call me mamma, some day?"
she whispered. " Not now;—when you feel
like it. I do not ask it till you feel like it."

" Yes,"— Matilda whispered in answer.

Presently Mrs. Laval began to tell her
about the ship fever, and the nursing, and
Miss Redwood; and how she and Miss Redwood had been alone with everything to do.
Then she wanted to hear how Matilda had
spent the weeks at the parsonage; and she
was very much amused.

" I believe I'll get you to teach me some
day," she said. " It's bad to be so helpless.
But I have learned something in these weeks.
Now, darling, is there anything you would
like, that I can give you? anything that
would be a pleasure to you? Speak and tell
me, before we go down to lunch."

The colour started into Matilda's face.

" If I could," she said,— " I would like, if
you liked it,—if Norton could go with me
again,—I would like *very* much, to go and
see Maria."

"Maria!" said Mrs. Laval. "At Poughkeepsie. Certainly. You shall go — let me
see, this is Monday, — Norton shall take you
Thursday. You must try and find something to take to Maria that she would like.
What would she like?"

Mrs. Laval was drawing out her purse.
Matilda, in a flush of delight, could not
think what Maria would like; so Mrs. Laval
gave her five dollars and bade her come to
her for more if she needed it.

Five dollars to buy Maria a present! Matilda went down to luncheon with her head
and her heart so full that she could hardly
eat. What should the present be? and what
a beginning of beautiful and delightful things
was this. She was as still as a mouse, and
eat about as much. Mrs. Laval and Norton
were full of business.

"How soon do we go to town, mamma?"

"As soon as possible! You ought to be
going to school. But — what day is it to-
day?"

" Monday, mamma."

" No, no; I mean what day of the month.
It is the middle of November, and past. I
can't go till the beginning of next month."

" Soon enough," said Norton. " Mamma,
is Pink to go to school ? "

Mrs. Laval looked at Matilda, smiled, but
made no answer.

" Mamma, let me teach her."

" You ? " said Mrs. Laval. " We will see."

" There's another thing. Mamma, is she
to have an allowance ? "

" Certainly."

" How much, mamma ? "

" As much as you have."

" Then she'll be rich," said Norton. " She
hasn't got boots to buy. My boots eat up
my money."

" I am afraid Matilda's boots will be quite
as troublesome to her. Don't you think she
will want boots ? "

" Girls' boots don't cost so much, do
they ? "

" It depends on where you get them."

" Mamma, Pink will not get her boots where you get yours, unless you give her the direction very carefully. She will think she must save the money for Lilac lane. You must take care of her, mamma; or she will think she ought to take a whole district on her hands, and a special block of old women."

Mrs. Laval again looked fondly at Matilda, and put a delicate bit on her plate, observing that she was not eating anything.

" You are to take her to Poughkeepsie Thursday, Norton, to see her sister."

" That's jolly," said Norton. " I want to be in Poughkeepsie, to see about some business of my own. We'll go to Blodgett's, Pink, and choose the hyacinths and tulips for our beds."

" You had a great deal better go to Vick, at Rochester," said Mrs. Laval. " You can depend upon what he gives you. I have not found Blodgett so careful."

"I should like to go to Mr. Vick's very much; but Rochester is rather too far off," said Norton.

"You can write, you foolish boy."

"Well," said Norton, "I believe that *will* be best. We cannot put the bulbs in now, unless we have a great stroke of good luck and there comes a soft bit of weather. I'll write to Vick. But we'll go to Blodgett's and get a few just for house blooming. Wouldn't you like that, Pink?

Matilda liked it so much that she found no words to express herself. Norton and his mother both laughed at her.

After dinner Mrs. Laval went with Matilda up to her room, and looked over her whole wardrobe. Most of the things which belonged to it Mrs. Laval threw aside; Matilda's old calico dresses and several of the others; and her old stockings and pocket handkerchiefs; and told Matilda she might give them away. New linen, she said, Matilda should have, as soon as she could get it made; meanwhile some new things were provided already. She bade Matilda take a bath; and then she had her own maid come in to arrange her hair and dress her. There was not much to be done with Matilda's hair; it was in short wavy locks all over her head; but the maid brushed it till Matilda thought she would never have done; and then she was dressed in a new dark brown merino, made short, and bound with a wide ribband sash; and new stockings were put on her that were gartered above her knees; and Matilda felt at once very nice and very funny. But when it was done, Mrs. Laval took her in her arms and half smothered her with caresses.

"We will get everything put in order, as soon as we get to New York," she said; "my rosebud! my pink, as Norton calls you; my Daphne blossom!"

"What is that, ma'am?" said Matilda laughing.

"Daphne? you shall have a plant of it, and

then you will know. It is something very
sweet, and yet very modest. It never calls
people to come and look at it."

She had Matilda on her lap; and she
stroked her hair, putting it back from her
brow; took her face in both hands and looked
at it and kissed it; played with her hands;
passed her fingers over the new stockings to
see how they fitted; tried the garters to see if
they were too tight; Matilda felt the touch of
motherly hands again, like no other hands.
It filled her with a warm gladness and sorrow, both together; but it bound her to Mrs.
Laval. She threw both arms at last around
her neck, and they sat so, wrapped up in each
other.

"You must go and call upon your aunt,
Matilda," Mrs. Laval said after a long silence.

"Must I? I suppose I must," said Matilda.

"Certainly. And the sooner you do it, the
more graceful it will be. I have been to see

her. So it is only necessary for you. It is a
proper mark of respect."

" I will go to-morrow ; shall I ? "

" Yes ; go to-morrow. Now Norton spoke
about an allowance. Would you like it ? "

" I don't know what it is, ma'am."

" I give Norton, that is, I *allow* him, five
dollars a month ; fifteen dollars a quarter.
Out of that he must provide himself with
boots and shoes and gloves ; the rest is for
whatever he wants, fish-hooks or hyacinths,
as the case may be. I shall give you the
same, Matilda ; five dollars every month.
Then I shall expect you to be always nicely
and properly dressed, in the matter of boots
and shoes and gloves, without my attending
to it. You are young to be charged with so
much care of your dress, but I can trust you.
With what is left of your allowance you will
do whatever you like ; nobody will ask any
questions about it. Do you like that, my
dear ? "

" Very much, ma'am."

" I thought so," said Mrs. Laval smiling.
" Now I want you to go with me and get
something to put on your head. I have had
a pelisse made for you that will do till we go
to the city and can find something better.
This can be then for second best. Put it on,
dear, and be ready; the carriage will be at
the door in a moment now."

Wondering, Matilda put on the pelisse.
She had never had anything so nice in her
life. It was of some thick, pretty, silver-grey
cloth, lined and wadded, and delicately
trimmed with silk. Then she went off with
Mrs. Laval in the carriage, and was fitted
with a warm little hat. Coming home
towards evening, at the close of this eventful
day, Matilda felt as if she hardly knew herself. To lay off her coat and hat in such a
warm, cheery little room, where the fire in
the grate bade her such a kind welcome; to
come down to the drawing-room, where
another fire shone and glowed on thick rugs
and warm-coloured carpets and soft cushions

and elegant furniture; and to know that she was at home amid all these things and comforts; it was bewildering. She sat down on a low cushion on the rug, and tried to collect her wits. What was it, she had resolved to do? — to watch for duty, and to do everything to the Lord Jesus? Then, so should her enjoyment of all this be. But Matilda felt as if she were taken off her feet. So she went to praying, for she could not think. She had only two minutes for that, before Norton rushed in and came to her side with Vick's Catalogue; and the whole rest of the evening was one delicious whirl through the wonders of a flower garden, and the beauties of various coloured hyacinths and tulips in particular.

The next day Matilda had two great matters on her heart; the present for Maria, and the visit to her aunt. She resolved to do the disagreeable business first. So she marched off to Mrs. Candy's in the middle of the morning, when she knew they were at leisure; and was ordered up into her aunt's room, where she and Clarissa were at work after the old fashion. The room had a dismal, oppressive air to Matilda's refreshed vision. Her aunt and cousin received each a kiss from her, rather than gave it.

"Well, Matilda," said Mrs. Candy, "how do you do?"

This, Matilda knew, was an introduction to something following. The answer was a matter of form.

"You've changed hands; how do you like it?" Mrs. Candy went on.

It would seem ungracious to say she liked it; so Matilda said nothing.

"I suppose things are somewhat different at Mrs. Laval's from what you found them here?"

"Yes, ma'am; they are different."

"Have Mrs. Laval's servants got quite well?"

"Yes, ma'am, quite well."

"How many of them are there?"

" There are the mother and father, and two daughters, and the brother of the father, I believe."

" And does Mrs. Laval keep other servants beside those ? "

" O yes.   Those are the farm servants, partly.   But one of them cooks, and one of the daughters is laundry maid ; and the other is the dairy woman."

" And how many more ? " asked Clarissa.

" There are the waiter and coachman, you know ; and the chambermaid ; and Mrs. Laval's own maid, and the sempstress."

" A sempstress constantly on hand ? " said Mrs. Candy.

" I believe so.   I have always seen her there.   She seems to belong there."

" Well, you find some difference between a house with a dozen servants, and one where they keep only one, don't you ? "

" It is different —" said Matilda, not knowing how to answer.

" What do *you* do, in that house with a dozen servants ? "

"I don't know, ma'am; I haven't done anything yet."

"How did you get among the sick people in the first place? how came that? It was very careless!"

"Nobody knew what was the matter with them, aunt Candy. Mrs. Laval was gone to town, and I went to take some beef tea that the doctor had ordered."

"Doctor Bird?"

"Yes."

"Doctor Bird ought to have known better. He ought to have taken better care," said Clarissa.

"It is easy to say that afterwards," remarked Mrs. Candy. "How came Mrs. Laval not to be there herself?"

"She was there. She was only gone to New York to get help; for all the servants had run away."

"Then *they* knew what was the matter," said Clarissa.

"I don't know," said Matilda. They

6

seemed frightened or jealous.   They all
went off."

"Like them," said Mrs. Candy.   "Who did
the nursing at last?"

"Mrs. Laval and Miss Redwood."

"Who is Miss Redwood?"

"She keeps house for Mr. Richmond."

A perceptible shadow darkened the faces
of both mother and daughter.   Matilda
wished herself away; but she could not end
her visit while it was yet so short; that
would not do.

"And so you have been wasting six weeks
at the parsonage, — doing absolutely nothing!"

It had not been precisely that.   But Matilda thought it was best to be silent.

"It seems to me you are not improving in
politeness," Mrs. Candy remarked.   "However, that is somebody else's affair now.
Are you going to school?"

"Not yet, ma'am."

"When are you going to begin?"

"I do not know. Not till we get to New York, I think."

"To New York! Then you are going to New York?"

"How soon?" Clarissa inquired.

"Not till next month."

"That is almost here," said Mrs. Candy. "Well, it would have been a great deal better for you to have remained here with me; but I am clear of the responsibility, that is one thing. If there is one thing more thankless than another, it is to have anything to do with children that are not your own. You know how to darn stockings, at any rate, Matilda; I have taught you that."

"And to mend lace," Clarissa added.

"Matilda may find the good of that yet. She may have to earn her bread with doing it. Nothing is more likely."

"I hope not," said Clarissa.

"It is an absurd arrangement anyhow," Mrs. Candy went on. "Matilda at Mrs. Laval's, and Anne and Letitia earning *their* bread with something not a bit better than mending lace. They will not like it very well."

" Why not, aunt Candy ?" Matilda asked.

" Wait and see if they do. Will they like it, do you think, to see that you do not belong to them any more and are part and parcel of quite another family ? Will they like it, that your business will be to forget them now? See if they like it !"

"Why I shall not forget them at all!" cried Matilda; "how could I? and what makes you say so ?"

" You are beginning by forgetting your mother," said Mrs. Candy, with a significant glance at the silver-grey pelisse.

" Yes," said Clarissa, " I noticed the minute she came in. How could Mrs. Laval do so !"

" What ?" said Matilda. " That isn't true at all, aunt Candy."

"I see the signs," said Mrs. Candy. " There is no need to tell me what they mean. In this country it is considered a mark of respect and a sign that we do not forget our friends, to wear a dress of remembrance."

" It reminds us of them, too," said Clarissa. " And we like to be reminded of those we love."

" I do not want anything to remind me of *her*," said Matilda; and the little set of her head at the moment spoke volumes. " And besides, aunt Candy and Clarissa, I did not wear mourning when I was here, except only when I went to church."

" That shewed the respect," said Mrs. Candy. " You can see easily what Mrs. Laval means, by her dressing you out in that style. Have you got a black dress under your coat?"

" Let us see what you have got," said Clarissa.

As Matilda did not move, Mrs. Candy rose and went to her and lifted up the folds of her pelisse so as to show the brown merino.

"I thought so," she remarked, as she went back to her seat.

"Mrs. Laval ought to be ashamed!" said her daughter.

Matilda had got by this time about as much as she could bear. She rose up from her uneasy chair opposite Mrs. Candy.

"O, are you going?" said that lady. "You do not care to stay long with us."

"Not to-day," said little Matilda, with more dignity than she knew, and with an air of the head and shoulders that very much irritated Mrs. Candy.

"I'd cure you of *that*," she said, "if I had you. I thought I had cured you. You would not dare hold your head like that, if you were living with me."

Now Matilda had not the least knowledge that her head was held differently from usual. She said good bye.

"Are you not going to kiss me?" said her aunt. "You are forgetting fast."

It cost an effort, but Matilda offered her

cheek to Mrs. Candy and to Clarissa, and left them. She ran down the stairs and out of the house. At the little gate she stood still.

What did it all mean? Forgetting her mother? Had she done her memory an injury, by putting on her brown frock and her grey pelisse? Was there any truth in all this flood of disagreeable words, which seemed to have flowed over and half drowned her. Ought her dress to be black? It had not been when she lived with her aunt, except on particular days and out of doors, as she had said. Was there any truth in all these charges? Matilda's heart had suddenly lost all its gayety, and the struggle in her thoughts was growing more and more unendurable every moment. A confusion of doubts, questions, suspicions which she could not at once see clearly enough to cast off, and sorrow, raged and fought in her mind with indignant rejection and disbelief of them. What should she do? How could she tell what was right? Mr. Richmond! She would go straight to him.

And so she did, hurrying along Butternut street like a little vessel in a gale; and she was just that, only the gale was in her own mind. It drove her on, and she rushed into the parsonage, excited by her own quick movements as well as by her thoughts. Miss Redwood was busy in the kitchen.

"What's the matter?" she exclaimed, for Matilda had gone in that way.

"I want to see Mr. Richmond."

"Well, he's in there. La! child, we keep open doors at the parsonage; there ain't no need that you should break 'em in by running against 'em. Take it easy, whatever there is to take. The minister's in his study. But his dinner'll be ready in a quarter of an hour, tell him."

Matilda went more quietly and knocked at the study door. She heard "Come in."

"Mr. Richmond, are you busy?" she asked, standing still inside of the study door.

" Shall I disturb you?" She was quiet
enough now. But the tears were shining in
Matilda's eyes, and the eyes themselves were
eager.

" Come here," said Mr. Richmond holding
out his hand; " I am not too busy, and your
disturbing me is very welcome. How do
you do?"

Matilda's answer was to clasp Mr. Richmond's hand and cover her face.

" What is the matter?" he asked softly,
though a little startled. " Nothing that we
cannot set right, Tilly?"

He drew his arm protectingly round her,
and Matilda presently looked up. " O Mr.
Richmond," she said, " I don't know if anything is wrong; but I want to know."

" Well, we can find out. What is the
question?"

" Mr. Richmond, the question is, Ought I
to wear black things for mamma?"

The minister was much surprised.

" What put this in your head, Tilly?"

" Mrs. Laval gave me some new dresses yesterday; these, you see, Mr. Richmond; the frock is dark brown and the coat is grey. Ought they to be black ? "

" Why should they be black ? "

" I don't know, sir. People do wear black things when they have lost friends."

" What for do they so ? "

" *I* don't know, Mr. Richmond ; but people say it shews respect — and that I do not shew " —

" Let us look at it quietly," said her friend. " How does it shew respect to a lost friend, to put on a peculiar dress? "

" I don't know, sir ; because it's the custom, I suppose. But I am not in black. Ought I to be ? "

" Wait; we will come to it. Black dresses are supposed to be a sign of grief, are they not ? "

" I don't know, Mr. Richmond ; they *said*, of respect, and to put one in mind."

" The grief that wants putting in mind, is

not a grief that pays much real respect, I should think. Do not you think so? that's one thing."

Matilda looked at him, with eyes intent and pitifully full of tears, just ready to run over, but eagerly watching his lips.

" Then as to respect, black dresses must shew respect, if any way, by saying to the world that we remember and are sorry. Now the fact is, Matilda, they do not say that at all. They are worn quite as much by people who do not remember, and who are not sorry. They tell nothing about the truth, except that some of those who wear them like to be in the fashion and some are afraid of what the world will say.

" But there is another question. When our friends have left us and are happy with the Lord Jesus, as all his children are, is it a mark of respect to their memory, that we should cover our faces with crape, and wear gloomy drapery, and shut up our shutters to keep the sunlight out of our rooms? Have we any right to stop the sunlight anywhere? Wouldn't it be better honour to our Christian friends who have gone, to be glad for them, and speak as if we were; and let it be seen that all the sorrow we have is on our own account, and we do not mean to indulge that selfishly? We do not sorrow as those that have no hope; for we believe that them which sleep in Jesus will God bring with him. There will be a glorious meeting again, by and by, when Jesus comes; then we and our dear ones who have loved him will be together again, and all of us with the Lord."

"Then people ought *not* to wear black for mourning?" said Matilda with a brightened but undecided face.

"I think myself it is a very unchristian fashion. It is not according to the spirit of the early Christian times; for people then who had had friends slain by wild beasts, and burned to death, for the truth of Jesus, gathered the poor remains that were left and laid them to rest, with the motto cut in the door of their resting place, — ' In peace. In Christ.' "

" Did they ! " said Matilda.

" A very great many of them."

" Then wouldn't you wear mourning, Mr. Richmond ? "

" I should not. I never have."

" Nor crape on your hat ? "

" Nor crape anywhere."

" Then I don't care ! " said Matilda.

" I do not think you need care."

" But it is very disagreeable ! " continued Matilda.

" What ? "

" That people will say such things."

Mr. Richmond smiled. " You must try and learn to bear that, Tilly. But it is not very difficult, when you are sure that you are in the right ? "

" I think it is difficult to bear," said Matilda.

" The only question is, what is right ? Do you remember the fairy tale, about the journey that a great many ladies and gentlemen took to the top of a hill, to get certain treasures that were there ? "

" The golden bird and the singing water ! " said Matilda. " Yes, I know. Do *you* know it, Mr. Richmond ? "

" I heard you telling it to Norton."

" I didn't know that you heard ! " said Matilda. " Well, Mr. Richmond ? — how could you remember ! "

" Well — if they looked round, when they were going up the hill, they lost all."

" They were turned into stone. And there were all sorts of noises in their ears, to make them look round."

" The only way to get to the top, was to stop their ears."

" Yes, Mr. Richmond; I know; I understand. But what golden bird and singing water are *we* going up hill after ? "

" Something better. We want the ' Well done, good and faithful servant,' — do we not? And if we would have that, we must stop our ears against all sorts of voices that would turn aside our eyes from what is at the top of the hill."

"But Mr. Richmond, it is not *wicked* to wear mourning, is it?"

"No. I was thinking then of other things. But it is very unlike the spirit of religion, when a friend has gone home, to make a parade of gloom about it; very unlike the truth of Christ."

"Mr. Richmond, I am very glad; and now I know what is right, I am very much obliged to you. And Miss Redwood said your dinner would be ready in a quarter of an hour. I guess it is ready now."

Which was the fact; and Matilda ran home, in a different sort of gale now, and at luncheon was quite as light hearted as usual.

CHAPTER IV.

IT was needful for Norton and Matilda, or they thought so, to take the early train which left the station at half past seven o'clock. The next train would not be till near eleven; and that, it was decided, would not do at all for their purposes. Taking the early train, they would have to go without breakfast; but that was no matter; they would get breakfast at Poughkeepsie, and have so much the more fun. The omnibus came for them a little after half past six, and they were ready; Matilda with an important basket on her arm, which Norton gallantly took charge of.

It was a delightful experience altogether. The omnibus did not immediately take the road to the station; there were several other passengers to gather up, and they drove round corners and stopped at houses in different streets of the village. First they took in old Mr. Kurtz; he was going to New York for his business, Norton whispered to Matilda; he had a large basket and an old lady with him. Then the omnibus went round into the street behind the parsonage and received Mr. Schönflocken, the Lutheran minister, and from another house another old lady with another basket. Two men got in from the corner. Lastly the omnibus stopped before a house near the baker's; and here they waited. The people were not ready. There were two children missing from the travelling party, it seemed. Inquiries and exclamations were bandied about; the stage driver knocked impatiently and cried out to hurry; Matilda was very much afraid they might miss the train. "Never mind; he knows his business," Norton remarked coolly. At last a man who had been in quest, brought back the stray children from an opposite lumber yard, calling out that they were found;

7

then there were kisses and leave takings,
and "Good bye, grandma!" and " Come back
again!"—and finally the mother put her children into the omnibus, the first, the second,
the third, and the fourth; then got in herself,
and the vehicle lumbered on. The omnibus
was crowded now; and the new comers had
been eating a breakfast of fried cakes and
fish, pretty near the stove where it was
cooked; for the smoke of the fry had filled
their clothes. Of course it filled the omnibus
also. This could be borne only a few minutes.

" Dear Norton," Matilda whispered, " can't
you open this window for me? I cannot
breathe."

" You'll catch cold," said Norton.

" No I won't. Please do! it is choking
me."

Norton laughed, and opened the window,
and Matilda putting her face close to the
opening was able to get a breath of fresh air.
Then she enjoyed herself again. The grey

dawn was brightening over the fields; the morning air was brisk and frosty; and as soon as Matilda's lungs could play freely again, so could her imagination. How pretty the dusky clumps of trees were against the brightening sky; how lovely . that growing light in the east, which every moment rose stronger and revealed more. The farm houses they passed looked as if they had not waked up yet; barns and farmyards were waiting for the day's work to begin; a waggoner or two, going slowly to the station, were all the moving things they saw. The omnibus passed them, and lumbered on.

"Norton," said Matilda suddenly, bringing her face round from the window, "it's delicious to be up so early."

"Unless you are obliged to take other people's breakfast before you get your own," said Norton. He looked disgusted, and Matilda could not help laughing in her turn.

"Put your nose to my window,—you can," she said. "The air is as sweet as can be."

" Outside " — grumbled Norton.

" Well, that is what I am getting," said Matilda. " Can't you get some of it ? — poor Norton ! "

" What I don't understand," said Norton, " is how people live."

At this point, the old woman with the basket got out, where a cross road branched off. Matilda was obliged to move up into the vacated place, to make more room for the others; and she lost her open window. However, the river came in sight now; the end of the ride was near; and soon she and Norton stood on the steps of the station house.

" I don't believe my coat will get over it all day," said the latter. " There ought to be two omnibuses."

" The poor people cannot help it, Norton; they are not to blame."

" Yes, they are," said Norton. " They might open their windows and air their houses. They are not fit to be in a carriage with clean people."

" I guess they don't know any better," said Matilda ; " and they were rather poor people, Norton."

" Well ? " said Norton. " That is what I say. There ought to be a coach for them specially."

He went in to buy the tickets, and Matilda remained on the steps, wondering a little why there should be poor people in the world. Why could not all have open windows and free air and sweet dresses ? Being poor, she knew, was somehow at the bottom of it ; and why should there be such differences ? And then, what was the duty of those better off ? " Whatsoever ye would that men should do to you," — that opened a wide field. Too big to be gone over just now. Matilda was sure that she was in the right way so far, in going to give pleasure to Maria ; and by the way she would take all the pleasure she could herself. How sweet it was now ! The sun was up, and shining with bright yellow light upon the hills of Rosendale and the opposite shore. The river was all in lively motion under the breeze; the ferry boat just coming in from Rondout; the sky overhead clearing itself of some racks of grey vapour and getting all blue. Could anything be more delicious? Now the passengers came trooping over from the " Lark," to get their tickets; and presently came the rumble of the train. She and Norton jumped into one of the cars, and then they were off.

" I'm hungry," was Norton's first confidence in the cars.

" So am I, very," said Matilda. " It will not take more than an hour, will it, to go to Poughkeepsie? "

" Not that," said Norton. " Then the very first thing will be, to go up to Smith's and get our breakfast."

" That's that restaurant? "

" Yes. A good one too."

" I never was in a restaurant in my life," said Matilda.

" We'll see how you like it, Pink; it's

delightful that you have never seen anything."

" Why ? "

" You have got so much to see. And I
want to know what you will think of it all."

Matilda was almost too happy. So happy,
that not a sunbeam, nor a ripple on the water,
nor a cloud in the sky, but seemed to bring
her more to be glad of. It was only that her
joy met these things and glanced back. So
Norton said. But Matilda thought it was
something beside.

" Why Norton, I am glad of those things
themselves," she insisted.

" Of the waves on the river ? " said Norton.

" Yes, to be sure I am."

" Nonsense, Pink! What for ? "

" I don't know what for," said Matilda.
" They are so pretty. And they are so lively.
And there is another thing, Norton," she said
with a change of voice. " God made them."

" Do you like everything he has made ? "
said Norton.

" I think I do."

" Then you must like those poor people in the omnibus, and poor people everywhere. Do *they* give you pleasure ? "

Matilda could not, say that they did. She wished with all her heart there were no such thing as poverty in the world. She could not answer immediately. And before she could answer the whistle blew.

" Is this Poughkeepsie ? "

" Yes, this is Poughkeepsie. Now we'll have breakfast !. Look sharp, Pink " —

In another minute, the two were standing on the platform of the station.

" Is *this* the place ? " Matilda inquired a little ruefully. She saw, inside the glass door, a large room with what seemed like a shop counter running down the length of it; and on this counter certainly eatables were set out; she could see cups of tea or coffee, and biscuits, and pieces of pie. People were crowding to this counter, and plates and cups seemed to have a busy time.

· · " This is Poughkeepsie," said Norton. " You have been here before. This our restaurant? I should think not! Not precisely. We have got to take a walk before we get to it. Smith's is at the top of the street."

" I am glad; I am ready to walk," said Matilda joyously; and they set off at a pace which shewed what sort of time their spirits were keeping. Nevertheless, all the way, between other things, Matilda was studying the problem of poverty which Norton had presented to her. The walk was quite a walk, and the footsteps were a little slower before the " top of the street " was reached. Why Norton called it so, Matilda did not see. The street went on, far beyond; but they turned aside round a corner, and presently were at the place they wanted.

They entered a nice quiet room, somewhat large, to be sure, and with a number of little tables set out; but nobody at any of them. Matilda and Norton went towards the back of the room, where it took an angle, and they could be a little more private. Here they took possession of one of the tables. Norton set down his basket, and Matilda took off her hat. Nothing, she thought, could possibly be any pleasanter than this expedition in which they were engaged. This was a rare experience; unparalleled.

"Now what shall we have?" said Norton.

"What *can* we have?" said Matilda.

"Everything. That is, any common thing. You couldn't get dishes of French make-ups, I suppose; and we don't want them. I am just as hungry as a bear."

"And I am as hungry as a bear*ess*."

Norton went off into a great laugh. "You look so like it!" he said. "But you might be as hungry as a bear; that don't say anything against your ladylike character. Though I always heard that she bears were fiercer than the others, when once they got their spirits up. Oh, Pink, Pink!" —

He was interrupted by the waiter.

" Now Pink, we've got to be civilized, and say what we'll have. You may have a cup of coffee."

" Yes, I would like it, Norton."

" And beefsteak? or cold chicken? We'll have chicken. I know you like it best."

It was nice of Norton; for he didn't.

" Buckwheats, Pink?"

" Yes. I like them," said Matilda.

" So do I, when they are good. And rolls, in case they shouldn't be. And good syrup — Silver Drip, mind."

Norton gave his order, and the two sat waiting. Matilda examined the place and its appointments. It was neat, if it was very plain.

" It's a good place enough," said Norton. " The country people come here in the middle of the day when they have driven in to Poughkeepsie to market and do shopping. Then the place is busy and all alive; now, you see, we have got it to ourselves. But anyhow, they have always good plain things here."

So the breakfast proved when it came. Matilda was very much amused with the little coffee pot, holding just enough for two, and the cream pitcher to match. But there was hot milk in plenty; and the cakes were feathery light; and the cold fowl very good; and the rolls excellent. And the two, Norton and Matilda, were very hungry. So much exercise and so much business and pleasure together made them sharp. Eating stopped talking a little. But the very goodness of the breakfast made Matilda think only the more, in the intervals, of that question Norton had given her; why were there poor people, who could have nothing like this?

"Shall we go to Blodgett's next? or will you see Maria first?" Norton asked.

"O, Maria first, Norton; and then we need not be hurried about the plants."

"The roots," said Norton. "Well, I'll see you there, and then I have some other business to attend to. I'll come for you about dinner time; then we can go to Blodgett's after dinner. You'll want a good deal of time with Maria, I suppose."

So after breakfast the two went down the town again and turned into the cross street where Maria lived. At the door of the humble-looking house, Norton left Matilda and went off again. Yes, it was a plain, small brick house, with wooden steps and little windows. Matilda had the door opened to her by Maria herself. She could not understand, though she surely saw, the cloud which instantly covered a flash of pleasure in Maria's face. The two went in, went up the stairs to a little back room, which was Maria's own. A chill came over Matilda here. It was so different from *her* room. A little close stove warmed it; the bed was covered with a gay patchwork quilt which had seen its best days; the chairs were but two, and those rush-bottomed. A painted wooden chest of drawers stood under the tiny bit of looking glass; the wash stand in the corner had but one towel thrown over it, and that not clean; one or two of Maria's dresses hung up against the wall. But a skirt of rich blue silk lay across the bed, for contrast; and yards of blue satin ribband lay partly quilled on the skirt, partly heaped on the patchwork quilt, and part had fallen on the floor. So one life touched another life.

"Well!" said Maria, for Matilda did not immediately begin what she had to say,— "how came you to be here so early?"

"We came down in the early train. I wanted to have a good long time to talk to you; and the next train is so late."

"Who came with you?"

"O, Norton. Norton Laval."

"Norton Laval! He came with you before. How came aunt Candy to let you come?"

"She could not help it."

"No," said Maria scornfully; "anything that Mrs. Laval wanted, she would say nothing against. She would go down on her knees, if she could get into Mrs. Laval's

house. Did Mrs. Laval ask her to get you
those new things?"

"No. Mrs. Laval"—

"How came she to do it, then?" interrupted Maria. "They are just as handsome
as they can be; and in the fashion too. But
she always liked you. I knew it. She never
gave *me* anything, but a faded silk necker-
chief. She is too mean"—

"O don't, Maria!" Matilda interrupted in
her turn. "Aunt Candy had nothing to do
with these things; she never gave me much
either; she did not get these for me."

"Who did, then?" said Maria opening her
eyes.

"Mrs. Laval."

"Mrs. Laval! How came *she* to do it?"

"Yes, Maria, because — Maria, I have gone
away from aunt Candy's."

"For a visit. I know. It has been a tremendously long visit, I think."

"Not for a visit now. Maria, I am not to
go back there at all any more; I mean, I am

not going back to aunt Candy. Mrs. Laval has taken me to keep — to be her own child. I am there now, for always."

"What?" Maria exclaimed.

"Mrs. Laval has taken me for her own, — for her own child."

"She hasn't!" said Maria; and if the wish did not point the expression, it was hard to tell what did. Matilda made no answer.

"Mrs. Laval has taken you? *for her own child?*" repeated Maria. "Do you mean that? To be with her, just like her own daughter? always?"

Matilda bowed her head, and her eyes filled. She was so disappointed.

"You aren't ever going to call her mamma? Don't you do it, Matilda! See you don't. If you do, I'll not be your sister any more. She shall not have that!"

Matilda was silent still, utterly dismayed.

"Why don't you speak? What made her do that, anyhow?"

"I don't know," said Matilda in a trembling voice. "She had a little daughter once, and she took me" — Matilda's eyes were glittering. She nearly broke down, but would not, and in the resistance she made to the temptation, her head took its peculiar airy turn upon her neck. Maria ought to have known her well enough to understand it.

"Everything comes to you!" she exclaimed. "I wonder why nothing comes to me! There are you, set up now, you think, above all your relations; you will not want to look at us by and by; I dare say you feel so now. And you are dressed, and have dresses made for you, and you ride in a carriage, and you have everything you want; and I here make dresses for other people, and live anyhow I can; sew and sew, from morning till night, and begin again as soon as morning comes; and never a bit of pleasure or rest or hope of it; and can't dress myself decently, except by the hardest! I don't know what I have done

8

to deserve it!" said Maria furiously. "It has always been so. Mamma loved you best, and aunt Candy treated you best, — she didn't love anybody; — and now strangers have taken you up; and nobody cares for me at all."

Here Maria completed her part of the harmony by bursting into tears. And being tears of extreme mortification and envy, they were hard to stop. The fountain was large. Matilda sat still, with her eyes glittering, and her head in the position that with her was apt to mean disapproval, and meant it now. But what could she say.

"It's very hard!"— Maria sobbed at last. "It's very hard!"

"Maria," said her little sister, "does it make it any harder for you, because I am taken such good care of?"

"Yes!" said Maria. "Why should good care be taken of you any more than of me? Of course it makes it harder."

There was nothing that it seemed wise to

say; and Matilda, sometimes a wise little child in her way, waited in silence, though very much grieved. She began to think it *was* hard for Maria, though the whole thing had got into a puzzle with her. And she thought it was a little bit hard for herself, that she should have taken such pains to prepare a present for her sister, and meet such a reception when she came to offer it.

"Just look what a place I live in!" sobbed Maria. "Not a nice thing about it. And here I sit and sew and sew, to make other people's things, from morning till night; and longer. I had to sit up till ten o'clock last night, puckering on that ribband; and I shall have to do it again to-night; till twelve, very likely; because I have spent time talking to you. All that somebody else may be dressed and have a good time."

"But Maria, what would you do if you *hadn't* this to do?" suggested Matilda.

"I don't know, and I don't care! I'd as lieve die as do this. I should like to put those pieces of blue ribband in the stove, and never see them again!"

"Isn't it pleasant work, Maria? I think it is pretty nice work. It isn't hard."

"Isn't it!" said Maria. "How would you like to try it? How would *you* like to exchange your room at Mrs. Laval's for this one? Haven't you got a nice room there?"

Matilda answered yes.

"How would you like to exchange it for this one, and to sit here making somebody's dress for a party, instead of riding about on the cars and going where you like and seeing everything and doing what you've a mind to? Nice exchange, wouldn't it be? Don't you think you'd like to try it? And I would come and see you and tell you how pleasant it is."

Matilda had nothing to say. Her eye glanced round again at the items of Maria's surroundings: the worn ingrain carpet; the rusty, dusty little stove; the patch-work counterpane, which the bright silk made to look so very coarse; and she could not but confess to herself that it would be a sore change to leave her pleasant home and easy life and come here. But what then?

" Maria, it isn't my fault," she said at last. " It is not my doing at all. And I think this is a *great* deal better than living with aunt Candy; and I would a great deal rather do it."

" I wouldn't," said Maria.

Matilda sat still and waited; her gayety pretty well taken down. She was very sorry for her sister, though she could not approve her views of things. Neither did she know well what to say to them. So she kept silence; until Maria stopped sobbing, dried her eyes, washed her hands, and began to quill her blue trimming again.

" What did you come to Poughkeepsie for, to-day? "

" To see you; nothing else."

" I think it is time. You haven't been here for weeks, and months, for aught I know."

" Because I wrote you why, Maria. There

was sickness at Briery Bank, and Norton and I were at the parsonage ever so long. I couldn't come to see you then."

" What have you got in that basket? your dinner? "

" O no; something that I wanted to shew to you. I wanted to bring you something, Maria; and I did not know what you would like; and I thought about it and thought about it all yesterday, and I didn't know. I wanted to bring you something pretty; but I remembered when I was here before you said you wanted gloves and handkerchiefs so much; and so, I thought it was better to bring you those."

While Matilda was making this speech, she was slowly taking out of her basket and unfolding her various bundles; she had half a hope, and no more now, that Maria would be pleased. Maria snatched the bundles, examined the handkerchiefs and counted them; then compared the gloves with her hand and laid them over it. Finally she put both gloves and handkerchiefs on the bed beside her, and went on sewing. She had not said one word about them.

" Are they right, Maria ? " said her little sister. " They are the right number, I know; do you like the colours I have chosen ? "

" They are well enough," Maria answered.

" Green and chocolate, I thought you liked," Matilda went on; "and the dark brown *I* liked. So I chose those. Do you like the handkerchiefs, Maria ? "

" I want them badly enough," said Maria. " Did you get them at Cope's ? "

" Yes, and I thought they were very nice. Are they ? "

"A child like you doesn't know much about buying such things," said Maria, quilling and turning her blue ribband with great energy. " Yes, they'll do pretty well. What sort of handkerchiefs have *you* got ? "

" Just my old ones. I haven't got any new ones."

I should like to see those, when you get

them. I suppose they'll be worked, and have lace round the borders."

" I shouldn't like it, if they had," said Matilda.

" We'll see, when you get them. I wonder how many things Anne and Letitia want? and can't get."

" I shall see them soon," said Matilda. " We are going to New York for the winter."

"You are!" exclaimed Maria, again ruefully. Matilda could not understand why. " But you won't see much of Anne and Letty, I don't believe."

" Perhaps I shall be going to school, and so not have much chance. Where do they live, Maria? I have forgotten."

" You will forget again," said Maria.

" But tell me, please. I will put it down."

" Number 316 Bolivar street. Now how much wiser are you?"

" Just so much," said Matilda, marking the number on a bit of paper. " I must know the name before I can find the place."

" You won't go there much," said Maria again. " Might just as well let it alone."

" Are the people here pleasant, Maria? are they good to live with?"

" They are not what you would call good."

" Are they pleasant? "

" No," said Maria. " They are not at all pleasant. I don't care who hears me say it. All the woman cares for, is to get as much work out of me as she can. That is how I live."

There was no getting to a smooth track for conversation with Maria. Begin where she would, Matilda found herself directly plunged into something disagreeable. She gave it up and sat still, watching the blue ribband curling and twisting in Maria's fingers, and wondering sadly anew why some people should be rich and others poor.

" Aren't you going to take off your things and have dinner with me?" said Maria, glancing up from her trimming.

" I cannot do that very well; Norton is coming for me; and I do not know how soon."

" I don't suppose I could give you anything you would like to eat.   Where will you get your dinner then ? "

" Somewhere with Norton."

" Then you didn't bring it with you ? "

" No."

Matilda did not feel that it would do to-day, to invite Maria to go with them to the restaurant.   Norton had said nothing about it; and in Maria's peculiar mood Matilda could not tell how she might behave herself or what she would say.   Perhaps Maria expected it, but she could not help that.   The time was a silent one between the sisters, until the expected knock at the house door came.   It was welcome, as well as expected. Matilda got up, feeling relieved if she felt also sorry; and after kissing Maria, she ran downstairs and found herself in the fresh open air, taking long breaths, like a person that had been shut up in a close little stove-heated

room. Which she had. And Norton's cheery
voice was a delightful contrast to Maria's dismal tones. With busy steps, the two went
up the street again to the restaurant. It was
pretty full of people now; but Norton and
Matilda found an unoccupied table in a corner. There a good dinner was brought them;
and the two were soon equally happy in eating it and in discussing their garden arrangements. After they had dined, Norton ordered
ice cream.

Matilda was as fond of ice cream as most
children are who have very seldom seen it; but
while she sat enjoying it she began to think
again, why she should have it and Maria not
have it? The question brought up the whole
previous question that had been troubling her,
about the rich and the poor, and quite gave
a peculiar flavour to what she was tasting.
She lost some of Norton's talk about
bulbs.

"Norton," she exclaimed at last suddenly,
"I have found it!"

" Found what?" said Norton. " Not a blue tulip?"

" No, not a blue tulip. I have found the answer to that question you asked me, — you know, — in the cars."

" I asked you five hundred and fifty questions in the cars," said Norton. " Which one?"

" Just before we got to Poughkeepsie, don't you remember?"

" No," said Norton laughing. " I don't, of course. What was it, Pink? The idea of remembering a question!"

" Don't you remember, you asked me if I didn't like poverty and poor people, for the same reason I liked other things?"

But here Norton's amusement became quite unmanageable.

" How *should* you like poverty and poor people for the same reason you like other things, you delicious Pink?" he said. " How should you like those smoky coats in the omnibus, for the same reason that you like a white hyacinth or a red tulip?"

" That is what I was puzzling. about, Norton; you don't recollect; and I could not make it out; because I knew I *didn't* enjoy poverty and poor things, and you said I ought."

" Excuse me," said Norton. " I never said you ought, in the whole course of my rational existence since I have known you."

" No, no, Norton; but don't you know, I said I liked everything, waves of the river and all, because God made them? and you thought I ought to like poor people and things for the same reason."

" O, that!" said Norton. " Well, why don't you?"

" That is what I could not tell, Norton, and I was puzzling to find out; and now I know."

" Well, why?"

" Because, God did *not* make them, Norton."

" Yes, he did. Doesn't he make everything?"

" In one way he does, to be sure ; but then, Norton, if everybody did just right, there would be no poor people in the world ; so it is not something that God has made, but something that comes because people won't do right."

" How ? " said Norton.

" Why Norton, you know yourself. If everybody was good and loved everybody else as well as himself, the people who have more than enough would give to the people who are in want, and there would not be uncomfortable poor people anywhere. And that is what the Bible says. ' He that hath two coats,' — don't you remember ? "

" No, I don't," said Norton. " Most people have two coats, that can afford it. What ought they to do ? "

" The Bible says, " let him impart to him that hath none.' "

" But suppose I cannot get another," said Norton ; " and I want two for myself ? "

" But somebody else has not *one?* suppose."

" I can very easily suppose it," said Norton. " As soon as we get out of the cars in New York I'll shew you a case."

"Well, Norton, that is what I said. If everybody loved those poor people, don't you see, they would have coats, and whatever they need. It is because you and I and other people *don't* love them enough."

" I don't love another boy well enough to give him my overcoat," said Norton. " But *coats* wouldn't make a great many poor people respectable. Those children in the omnibus this morning had coats on, comfortable enough; the trouble was, they were full of buckwheat cake smoke."

" Well if people are not clean, that's their own fault," said Matilda. " But those people this morning hadn't perhaps any place to be in *but* their kitchen. They might not be able to help it, for want of another room and another fire."

Matilda was eager, but Norton was very much amused. He ordered some more ice cream and a charlotte. Matilda eat what he gave her, but silently carried on her thoughts; *these* she would have given to Maria, if she could; she was having more than enough.

Moralizing was at an end when she got to the gardener's shop. · The consultations and discussions which went on then, drove everything else out of her head. The matter in hand was a winter garden, for their home in New York.

" I'll have some auriculas this year," said Norton. " You wouldn't know how to manage them, Pink. You must have tulips and snowdrops; O yes, and crocuses. You can get good crocuses here. And polyanthus narcissus you can have. You will like that."

" But what will you have, Norton ? "

" Auriculas. That's one thing. And then, I think I'll have some Amaryllis roots — but I won't get those here. I'll get tulips and hyacinths, Pink."

" Shall we have room for so many ? "

" Lots of room. There's my room has two

south windows — that's the good of being on a corner; and I don't know exactly what your room will be, but I'll get grandmother to let us live on that side of the house any- how. Nobody else in the family cares about a south window, only you and I. Put up a dozen Van Tols, and a dozen of the hyacinths, and three polyanthus narcissus, and a dozen crocuses; — and a half dozen snowdrops."

" Will you plant them while we are in Shadywalk ? "

" Of course," said Norton ; " or else they'll be blossoming too late, don't you see ? Un- less we go to town very soon; and in that case we'll wait and keep them."

The roots were paid for and ordered to be sent by express; and at last Norton and Ma- tilda took their journey to the station house to wait for the train. It was all a world of delight to Matilda. She watched eagerly the gathering people, the busy porters and idle hack drivers; the expectant table and waiters in the station restaurant; every detail

9

and almost every person she saw had the charm of novelty or an interest of some sort for her unwonted eyes. And then came the rumble of the train, the snort and the whistle; and she was seated beside Norton in the car, with a place by the window where she could still watch everything. The daylight was dying along the western shore before they reached the Shadywalk station; the hills and the river seemed to Matilda like a piece of a beautiful vision; and all the day had been like a dream.

CHAPTER V.

IT was near dark by the time they got home, and Matilda was tired. Tea and lights and rest were very pleasant; and after tea she sat down on a cushion by Mrs. Laval's side, while Norton told over the doings of the day.

"Which room will Matilda have, mamma, in New- York?" Norton asked.

"I don't know. Why are you anxious?"

"We want south windows for our plants."

"She shall have a south window," said Mrs. Laval fondly. "And I have had a letter from your grandmother, Norton. I think I shall go to town next week."

"Before December!" cried Norton. "Hurra! That is splendid. After we get into December and I am going to school, the days and the weeks get into such a progress that they trip each other up, and I don't know where I am. And there's Christmas. Mamma, don't send Pink to school! Let me teach her."

"I don't think you know very well where you are now," said his mother smiling. "What will you do with your own lessons?"

"Plenty of time," said Norton. "Too much time, in fact. Mamma, I don't think Pink would enjoy going to school."

"We will see," Mrs. Laval said. "But there is something else Pink would enjoy, I think. You have not got your allowance yet, Matilda. Have you a purse, love? or a porte-monnaie, or anything?"

"O yes, ma'am! Don't you remember, ma'am, you gave me *your* pocket book? a beautiful red morocco one, with a sweet smell?"

"No," said Mrs. Laval laughing.

"It was before the sickness — O, long ago; you gave it to me, with money in it, for Lilac lane."

" Is the money all gone ? "

" It is all gone," said Matilda; "for you remember, Mrs. Laval, Norton and I had a great many things to get for that poor woman and her house. It took all the money."

" You had enough ? "

" O yes, ma'am; Norton helped."

" Well then you have a pocket book; that will serve to hold your future supplies. I shall give you the same as I give Norton, five dollars a month; that is fifteen dollars a quarter. Out of that you will provide yourself with boots and shoes and gloves; you may consult your own taste, only you must be always nice in those respects. Here is November's five dollars."

" Mamma, November is half out," said Norton.

" Matilda has everything to get; she has to begin without such a stock as you have on hand."

" Mamma, you will give her besides for her Christmas presents, won't you ? "

" Certainly.   As I do you."

" How much will you give her, mamma? For I foresee we shall have a great deal of work to attend to in New York stores before Christmas; and Matilda will naturally want to know how much she has to spend."

" She can think about it," said Mrs. Laval smiling. " You do not want your Christmas money yet."

"We shall get into great trouble," said Norton with a mock serious face. " I foresee I shall have so much advising to do — and to take — that it lies like a weight on me. I can't think how Pink will settle things in her mind.   At present she is under the impression that she must not keep more than one pair of boots at a time."

" You want several, my darling," said Mrs. Laval, " for different uses and occasions. Don't you understand that ? "

" Yes ma'am, I always did " —

Matilda would have explained, but Norton broke in. " She thinks two overcoats at once is extravagant, mamma; I ought to give one of them away." .

Matilda wanted to say that Norton was laughing, and yet what he said was partly true. She held her peace.

" You do not really think that, my darling," said Mrs. Laval, putting her arm round Matilda, and bending down her face for a kiss. " You do not think that, do you ? "

It was very difficult to tell Mrs. Laval what she really did think. Matilda hesitated.

" Don't you see," said the lady, laughing and kissing her again, " don't you see that Norton wants two overcoats just as much as he wants one ? The one he wears every day to school would not be fit to go to church in. Hey ? " said Mrs. Laval with a third kiss.

" Mamma, there are reasons against all that; you do not understand," said Norton.

" It's very hard to say," Matilda spoke at length, rousing herself; for her head had gone down on Mrs. Laval's lap. " May I say exactly what I do mean ? "

" Certainly ; and Norton shall not interrupt you."

" I don't want to interrupt her," said Norton. " It is as good as a book."

" What is it, my love ? "

Matilda slipped off her cushion and kneeling on the rug, with her hands still on Mrs. Laval's lap, looked off into the fire.

" The Bible says " — she began and checked herself. The Bible was not such authority there. " I was only thinking — Ma'am, you know how many poor people there are in the world ? "

" Yes, dear."

" *She* doesn't," said Norton.

" People that have no overcoats at all, nor under coats neither, some of them. I was thinking — if *all* the people who have plenty, would give half to the people who have nothing, there would be nobody cold or miserable ; I mean, miserable from *that*."

" Yes, there would, my darling," said Mrs. Laval. " People who are idle and wicked, and won't work and do not take care of what they have, they would be poor if we were to give them, not half but three quarters, of all we have. It would be all gone in a week or two; or a month or two."

Matilda looked at Mrs. Laval. " But the poor people are not always wicked ? "

" Very often. Industrious and honest people need never suffer."

That would alter the case, Matilda thought. She sat back on her cushion again and laid her head down as before. But then, what meant the Bible words; " He that hath two coats, let him impart to him that hath none; and he that hath meat, let him do likewise "? The Bible could not be mistaken. Matilda was puzzled with the difficult question; and presently the warm fire and her thoughts together were too much for her. The eyelids drooped over her eyes ; she was asleep. Mrs. Laval made a sign to Norton to keep quiet. Her own fingers touched tenderly the soft brown locks of the head which lay on her lap; but too softly to disturb the sleeper.

" Mamma," said Norton softly, " isn't she a darling ? "

" Hush ! " said Mrs. Laval. " Don't wake her."

" She is perfectly fast asleep," said Norton. " She don't sham sleeping any more than awake.   Mamma, how will grandmamma like her ? "

" She cannot help it," said Mrs. Laval.

" Aunt Judy won't," said Norton.   " But mamma, she is twenty times prettier than Judith Bartholomew."

" She is as delicate as a little wood flower," said Mrs. Laval.

" She has more stuff than *that*," said Norton; " she is stiff enough to hold her head up; but I'll tell you what she is like.   She is like my Penelope hyacinth."

" Your Penelope hyacinth ! " Mrs. Laval echoed.

" Yes ; you do not know it, mamma.   It is

not a white hyacinth; just off that; the most delicate rose pearl colour. Now Judy is like a purple dahlia."

"Matilda is like nothing that is not sweet," said Mrs. Laval fondly, looking at the little head.

"Well, I am sure hyacinths are sweet," said Norton. "Mamma, will you let me teach her?"

"You will not have time."

"I will. I have plenty of time."

"What will you teach her?"

"Everything I learn myself — if you say so."

"Perhaps she would like better to go to school."

"She wouldn't," said Norton. "She likes everythiug that I say."

"Does she!" said his mother laughing. "That is dangerous flattery, Norton."

"Her cheeks are just the colour of the inside of a pink shell," said Norton. "Mamma, there is not a thing ungraceful about her."

" Not a thing," said Mrs. Laval. " Not a movement."

" And she is so dainty," said Norton. " She is just as particular as you are, mamma."

" Or as my boy is," said his mother, putting her other hand upon his bright locks. " You are my own boy for that."

" Mamma," Norton went on, " I want you to give Pink to me."

" Yes, I know what that means," said his mother. " That will do until you get to school and are going on skating parties every other day; then you will like me to take her off your hands."

Norton however did not defend himself. He kissed his mother, and then stooped down and kissed the sleeping little face on her lap.

" Mamma, she is so funny!" he said. " She actually puzzles her head with questions about rich and poor people, and the reforms there ought to be in the world; and she thinks she ought to begin the reforms, and I ought to carry them on. It's too jolly."

"It will be a pleasure to see her pleasure in New York."

"Yes, won't it! Mamma, nobody is to take her first to the Central Park but me."

The questions about rich and poor were likely to give Matilda a good deal to do. She had been too sleepy that night to think much of anything; but the next day, when she was putting her five dollars in her pocketbook, they weighed heavy.

"And this is only for November," she said to herself; "and December's five dollars will be here directly; and January will bring five more. Fifteen. How many shoes and boots must I get for that time?"

Careful examination shewed that she had on hand one pair of boots well worn, another pair which had seen service as Sunday boots, but were quite neat yet, and one pair of nice slippers. The worn boots would not do to go out with Mrs. Laval, nor anywhere in

company with Matilda's new pelisse. "They
will only do to give away," she concluded.
They would have seen a good deal of service
in Shadywalk, if she had remained there with
her aunt Candy; Mrs. Laval was another
affair.   One pair for every day and one pair
for best, would do very well, Matilda thought.
Then gloves? She must get some gloves.
How many?

She went to Mr. Cope's that very afternoon, and considered all the styles of gloves
he had in his shop. Fine kid gloves, she
found, would eat up her money very fast.
But she must have them; nothing else could
be allowed to go to church or anywhere in
company with Mrs. Laval, and even Norton
wore nothing else when he was dressed.
Matilda got two pair, dark brown and dark
green; colours that she knew would wear
well; though her eyes longed for a pair of
beautiful tan colour. But besides these, Matilda laid in some warm worsted gloves, which
she purposed to wear in ordinary or whenever

she went out by herself. She had two dollars left, when this was done. The boots, Mrs. Laval had told her, she was to get in New York; she could wait till December for them.

And now everybody was in a hurry to get to New York. The house was left in charge of the Swiss servants. The grey ponies were sent down the river by the last boat from Rondout. Matilda went to see Mrs. Eldridge once, during these days of bustle and expectancy; and the visit refreshed all those questions in her mind about the use of money and the duties of rich people. So much work a little money here had done! It was not like the same place. It was a humble place doubtless, and would always be that; but there was cozy warmth instead of desolation; and comfortable tidiness and neatness instead of the wretched condition of things which had made Matilda's heart sick once; and the poor woman herself was decently dressed, and her face had brightened up wonderfully.

Matilda read to her, and came away glad and thoughtful.

The farewell visit was paid at the parsonage the last thing; and on the first of December the party set out to go to the new world of the great city. It was a keen, cold winter's day; the sky bleak with driving grey clouds; the river rolling and turbulent under the same wind that sped them. Sitting next the window in the car, where she liked to sit, Matilda watched it all with untiring interest; and while she watched it, she thought by turns of Mr. Richmond's words the evening before. Matilda had asked him how she should be sure to know what was right to do always? Mr. Richmond advised her to take for her motto those words — " Whatsoever ye do, in word or deed, do all in the name of the Lord Jesus;" — and to let every question be settled by them. He said they would settle every one, if she was willing they should. And now as Matilda sat musing, she believed they would; but a doubt came up, — if she lived by that rule, and all around her without exception went by another rule, how would they get along? She was obliged to leave it; she could not tell; only the doubt came up.

It seemed a long way to New York. After Poughkeepsie had been some time left behind, Matilda began to think it was time to hear about the end of the journey; but Norton told her they were only in the Highlands. Matilda watched the changing shores, brown and cold-looking, till the hills were left behind, and the river took a look she was more accustomed to. Still Norton only laughed at her, when she appealed to him; they were not *near* New York, he said; it was Haverstraw bay. It seemed to take a great while to pass that bay and Tappan Sea. Then Norton pointed out to her the high straight line of shore on the opposite side of the river. " Those are the Palisades, Pink," he said; "and when you see the Palisades come to an end, *then* New York is not far off."

10

But it seemed as if the Palisades would never come to an end, in Matilda's tired fancy. She was weary of the cars by this time, and eager for the sight of the new strange place where her life was to be for so long. And the cars sped on swiftly, and still the straight line of the Palisades stretched on too. At last, at last, that straight line shewed signs of breaking down.

"Yes," said Norton, to whom Matilda pointed this out, — "we'll soon be in now, Pink."

Matilda roused up, to use her eyes with fresh vigilance. She noticed one or two places where carts and men were busy, seemingly, with the endeavour to fill up the North river; at least they were carrying out loads of earth and dumping it into the water. She was tired of talking by this time, and waited to ask an explanation till the roar of the car-wheels should be out of her ears. They came to scattered buildings; then the buildings seemed less scattered; then the train

slackened its wild rate of rushing on, and
Matilda could better see what she was passing. They were in a broad street at last,
broader than any street in Shadywalk. But
it was dismal! Was this New York? Matilda had never seen such forlorn women and
children on the sidewalks at home. Nor ever
so much business going on there. Everybody
was busy, except one or two women lounging
in a doorway. Carts, and builders, and hurried passers by; and shops and markets and
grocery stores in amazing numbers and suc-
cession. But with a sort of forlornness about
them. Matilda thought she would not like
to have to eat the vegetables or the meat she
saw displayed there.

Then came the slow stopping of the cars;
and the passengers turned out into the long
shed of the station house. Here Norton left
them, to go and find the carriage; while Matilda lost herself in wonder at the scene. So
many people hurrying off, meeting their
friends, hastening by in groups and pairs,

and getting packed into little crowds; such
numbers of coachmen striving for customers
at the doors, with their calls of " Carriage,
sir ? " " Carriage, ma'am ? " pattering like
hail. It was wonderful, and very amusing.
If this was only the station house of the rail-
way, and the coming in of one train, Matilda
thought New York must be a very large
place indeed. Presently Norton came back
and beckoned them out, through one of those
clusters of clamorous hackney coachmen, and
Matilda found herself bestowed in the most
luxurious equipage she had ever seen in her
life. Surely it was like nothing but the appointments of fairy land, this carriage. Matilda sunk in among the springs as if they had
been an arrangement of feathers; and the
covering of the soft cushions was nothing
worse than satin, of dark crimson hue.
Nothing but very handsome dresses could go
in such a carriage, she reflected; she would
have to buy an extremely neat pair of boots to
go with the dresses or the carriage either. It

was Mrs Lloyd's carriage; and Mrs. Lloyd was Mrs. Laval's mother.

The carriage was the first thing that took Matilda's attention; but after that she fell to an eager inspection of the houses and streets they were passing through. These changed rapidly, she found. The streets grew broad, the houses grew high; groceries and shops were seldomer to be seen, and were of much better air; markets disappeared; carmen and carts grew less frequent; until at last all these objectionable things seemed to be left behind, and the carriage drew up before a door which looked upon nothing that was not stately. Up and down, as far as Matilda could see, the street was clean and splendid. She could see this in one glance, almost without looking, as she got out of the carriage, before Norton hurried her in.

She felt strange, and curious; not afraid; she knew the sheltering arms of her friends would protect her. It was a doubtful feeling, though, with which she stepped on the mar-

ble floor of the hall and saw the group which
were gathered round Mrs. Laval. What
struck Matilda at first was the beautiful hall,
or room she would have called it, though the
stairs went up from one side ; its soft warm
atmosphere ; the rustle of silks and gleam of
colours, and the gentle bubbling up of voices
all around her. But she stood on the edge
of the group. Soon she could make more
detailed observations.

That stately lady in black silk and lace
shawl, she was Mrs. Laval's mother; she
heard Mrs. Laval call her so. Very stately,
in figure and movement too ; a person accustomed to command and have her own way,
Matilda instinctively felt. Now she had her
arms round Norton ; she was certainly very
fond of him. The lady with lace in her
gleaming hair, and jewels at her breast, and
the dress of crimson satin falling in rich folds
all about her, sweeping the marble, that must
be Mrs. Laval's sister. She looked like a
person who did not do anything and had not

anything she need do, like Mrs. Laval.
Then this girl of about her own age, with a
very bright mischievous face and a dress of
sky blue, Matilda knew who she must be;
would they like each other, she questioned?
And then she had no more time for silent
observations; Norton called upon her, and
pulled her forward into the group.

" Grandmamma, you have not seen her,"
he cried; "you have not seen one of us.
This is mamma's pet, and my — darling."
It was evident the boy's thought was of
" daughter " and " sister," but that a tender
feeling stopped his tongue. Mrs. Lloyd looked
at Matilda.

" I have heard of her," she said.

" Yes, but you must kiss her. She is one
of us."

" She is *mine*," said Mrs. Laval meaningly,
putting both arms around Matilda and drawing her to her mother.

The stately lady stooped and kissed the
child, evidently because she was thus asked.

" Grandmamma, she is to have half my place in your heart," said Norton.

" Will you give it up to her?" Mrs. Lloyd asked.

" It is just as good as my having it," said Norton.

Perhaps he would have presented Matilda then to his aunt, but that lady had turned off into the drawing room; and the travellers mounted the stairs with Mrs. Lloyd to see their apartments and to prepare for dinner. The ladies went into a large room opening from the upper hall; Norton and the girl Matilda had noticed went bounding up the second flight of stairs.

Mrs. Laval lay down on a couch, and said she would have a cup of tea before dressing. While she took it, Mrs. Lloyd sat beside her and the two talked very busily. Matilda, left to herself, put off her coat and hat and sat down at the other side of the fire, for a fire was burning in the grate, and pondered the situation. The house was like a palace in a fairy tale, surely, she thought. Her eyes were dazzled with the glimmer from gildings and mirrors and lamps hanging from the ceilings. Her foot fell on soft carpets. The hangings of the bed were of blue silk. The couches were covered with rich worsted work. Pictures made the walls dainty. Beautiful things which she could not examine yet, stood on the various tables. It immediately pressed on Matilda's attention, that to be of a piece with all this elegance and not out of place among the people inhabiting there, she had need to be very elegant herself. The best dress in her whole little stock was the brown merino she had worn to travel in. She had thought it very elegant in Shadywalk; but how did it look alongside of Miss Judy's blue silk? Matilda had nothing better, at any rate. She glanced down at her boots, to see how they would do. They were her best Sunday boots. They were neat, she concluded. They wanted a little brushing from dust; then they would do pretty well. But she did not think they were elegant. The soles of them were rather too thick for that. At this point her attention was drawn to what was saying at the other side of the fire.

" Do the children dine with us? "

" To-day."

" Not in ordinary ? "

"It is bad for the boys; puts them out. One o'clock suits them a great deal better. And six is a poor hour for children always. And with company of course it is impossible; and that makes irregularity; and *that* is bad."

" I suppose it is best so," said Mrs. Laval with half a sigh. " What room is Matilda to have, mother? "

" Matilda ? — O, your new child. You want her to have a room to herself? "

" Yes."

" I will let her have the little front corner room, if you like. There is room enough."

" That will do," said Mrs. Laval. " Come,

darliug, let us go upstairs and look at it.
Then you will begin to feel at home."

She sprang off the sofa, and taking Matilda's hand they mounted together the
second flight of stairs; wide, uncarpeted,
smooth, polished stairs they were; to the upper hall. Just at the head of the stairs Mrs.
Laval opened a door. It let them into a
pretty little room; little indeed only by comparison with other larger apartments of the
house; it was of a pleasant size, with two
great windows; and being a corner room, its
windows looked out in two directions, over
two several city views. Matilda had no time
to examine them just then; her attention was
absorbed by the room. It had a rich carpet;
the hangings and covering of the bed were
dark green; an elegant little toilet table was
furnished with crystal, and the washcloset
had painted green china dishes. There were
pictures here too, and little foot cushions, and
a beautiful chest of drawers, and a tall wardrobe for dresses. The room was full.

This will do very nicely," said Mrs. Laval. " You wanted a south window, Matilda; here it is. I think you will like this room better than one of those large ones, darling; they are large enough for you to get lost in. See, here is the gas jet, when you want light; and here are matches, Matilda. And now you will have a place where you can be by yourself when you wish it; and at other times you can come down to me. You will feel at home, when you get established here, and have some dresses to hang up in that wardrobe. That is one of the first things you and I must attend to. I could not do it at Shadywalk. So come down now, dear, to my room, and we will get ready for dinner. Are you tired, love ? "

Matilda met and answered the kiss that ended this speech, and went downstairs again a very contented child. However, all her getting ready for dinner that day consisted in a very thorough brushing of her short hair, and a little furtive endeavour to get rid of some specks of dust on her boots. She sat down then and waited, while Mrs. Laval changed her travelling dress, and Mrs. Bartholomew alternately assisted and talked to her. That elegant crimson satin robe swept round the room in a way that was very imposing to Matilda. She could not help feeling like a little brown thrush in the midst of a company of resplendent parrots and birds of paradise. But she did not much care. Only she thought it would be very pleasant to have the wardrobe upstairs furnished with a set of dresses to correspond somewhat with her new splendid surroundings. Mrs. Bartholomew had not spoken to her yet, nor anybody, except Mrs. Laval's mother. Matilda thought herself forgotten; but when the ladies were about to go downstairs, Mrs. Laval called her sister's attention to the subject.

"Judith, this is my new child."

Mrs. Bartholomew cast a comprehensive glance at Matilda, or all over her. Matilda

could not have told whether she had looked
at her until then.

" Where did you pick her up, Zara ? "

"I did not pick her up," said Mrs. Laval,
smiling at Matilda. " A wave wafted her
into my arms."

" What sort of a wave ?" said the other
lady dryly.

" No matter what sort of a wave. You
see from what sort of a shore this flower
must have drifted."

" You are poetical," said the other, laughing slightly. " You always were. Shall we
go down ? "

Mrs. Laval stretched out her hand to Matilda and held it in a warm clasp as they
went down the stairs; and still held her fast
and seated her by herself in the drawing
room. It was the only point of connection
with the rest of the world that Matilda felt
she had just then. Until Norton came running downstairs with his two cousins, and
entered the room.

" Come here, Judy," said Mrs. Laval.
" This is my new little daughter, Matilda.
You two must be good cousins and friends."

Miss Black-eyes took Matilda's hand; but
somehow Matilda could perceive neither the
friendship nor the cousinship in the touch
of it.

" Matilda what ? " Miss Judith asked. Her
aunt hesitated an instant.

" She has not learned yet to do without
her old name. Her new name is mine, of
course."

Matilda was a good deal startled and a
little dismayed. Was she to give up her own
name then, and be called Laval? she had
not heard of it before. She was not sure
that she liked it at all. There was no time
to think about it now.

" David," Mrs. Laval went on, " come here.
I want you all to be good friends as soon as
possible."

She put Matilda's hand in his as she spoke.
But David said never a word ; only he bowed

over Matilda's hand in the most calmly polite manner, and let it drop.   He was not shy,
Matilda thought, or he could not have made
such an elegant reverence; but he did not
speak a word.   His aunt laughed a little, and
yet gave a glance of admiration at the boy.

"You are not changed," she said.

Changed in what? Matilda wondered; and
she looked to see what she could make out
in David Bartholomew.   He was not so dark
as his sister; he had rich brown hair; and
the black eyes were not snapping and spark-
ling like hers, but large, lustrous, proud, and
rather gloomy, it seemed to the little stranger's fancy.   She looked away again; she did
not like him.   In another minute they were
called to dinner.

It was but to walk across the hall, and
Matilda found herself seated at the most imposing board she had ever beheld.   Certainly
everything at Mrs. Laval's table was beautiful and costly; but there it had been only a
table for two or three; no company, and the

simplest way of the house. Here there was a good tableful, and a large table; and the sparkle of glass and silver quite dazzled the child's unaccustomed eyes. How much silver, and what brilliant and beautiful glass! She wondered at the profusion of forks by her own plate, and almost thought the waiter must have made a mistake; but she saw Norton was as well supplied. The lights, and the flowers, and the fruit in the centre of the table, and the gay silks and laces around it, and all the appointments of the elegant room, almost bewildered Matilda. Yet she thought it was very pleasant too, and extremely pretty; and discovered that eating dinner was a great deal more of a pleasure when the eyes could be so gratified at the same time with the taste. However, soup was soup, she found, to a hungry little girl.

"Pink," said Norton, after he had swallowed *his* soup, — "where do you think we will go first?" Norton had got a seat beside her and spoke in a confidential whisper.

11

" I am going with your mother to-morrow,"
Matilda returned in an answering whisper.
" So she said."

" That won't tire you out," said Norton.
" After she goes, or before she goes, you and
I will go.   Where first ? "

" You and I alone ? " said Matilda softly.

" Alone ! "

" Norton," said Matilda very softly, " I
think I want to go first of all to the shoemaker's."

Norton had nearly burst out into a laugh,
but he crammed his napkin against his
face.

" You dear Pink ! " he said ; " that isn't
anywhere.   That's business.   I mean pleasure.   You see, next week I shall begin to go
to school, and my time will be pretty nicely
taken up, except Saturday.   We have got
three days before next week.   And you have
got to see everything."

" But Norton, I do not know what there is
to see."

" That's true. You don't, to be sure.
Well Pink, there's the Park; but we must
have a good day for that; to-day is so cold it
would bite our noses. We can go every
afternoon, if it's good. Then there is the
Museum; and there is a famous Menagerie
just now."

" Oh Norton !" — said Matilda.

" Well ? "

" Do you mean a Menagerie with lions ?
and an elephant ? "

" Lions, and splendid tigers, David says;
and an elephant, and a hippopotamus; and
ever so many other creatures besides. All of
them splendid, David says."

" I did not use that word," David remarked
from the other side of the table.

" All right," said Norton. " It is my word.
Then, Pink, we'll pay our respects to the
lions and tigers the first thing. After the
shoe " —

" Hush, Norton," said Matilda. " You forget yourself."

Norton laughed, pleased; for Matilda's little head had taken its independent set upon her shoulders, and it shewed him that she was feeling at ease, and not shy and strange, as he had feared she might. In truth the lions and tigers had drawn Matilda out of herself. And now she was able to enjoy roast beef and plum pudding and ice cream as well as anybody, and perhaps more; for to her they were an unusual combination of luxuries. Now and then she glanced at the other people around the table. Mrs. Lloyd always seemed to her like a queen; the head of the house; and the head of such a house was as good as a queen. Judith looked like a young lady who took, and could take, a great many liberties in it. David, like a grave, reserved boy who never wanted to take one. Mrs. Bartholomew seemed a luxurious fine lady; · Matilda's impression was that she cared not much for anybody or anything except herself and her children. And how rich they all must be! Not Mrs. Lloyd alone; but all these. Their dress shewed it, and their talk, and their air still more. It was the air of people who wanted nothing they could not have, and did not know what it meant to want anything long. Mrs. Lloyd was drinking one sort of wine, Mrs. Bartholomew another, and Mrs. Laval another; one had a little clear wineglass, another a yellow bowl-like goblet, much larger; the third had a larger still. Every place was provided with the three glasses, Matilda saw. Just as her observations had got thus far, she was startled to see Norton sign the servant and hold his claret glass to be filled.

Matilda's thoughts went into a whirl immediately. She had not seen Norton take wine at home; it brought trooping round her, by contrast, the recollections of Shadywalk, the Sunday school room, the meetings of the Commission, and Mr. Richmond, and talk about temperance, and her pledge to do all she could to help the cause of temperance. Now, here was a field. Yes, and there was

David Bartholomew on the other side of the table, he also was just filling his glass. But what could Matilda do here? Would these boys listen to her? And yet, she had promised to do all she could for the cause of temperance. She could certainly do something, in the way of trying at least. She must. To try, is in everybody's power. But now she found as she thought about it, that it would be very difficult even to try. It is inconceivable how unwilling she felt to say one word to Norton on the subject; and as for David! — Well, she need not think of David at present; he was a stranger. If she could get Norton to listen — But she could not get Norton to listen, she was sure; and what was the use of making a fuss and being laughed at just for nothing? Only, she had promised.

The working of these thoughts pretty well spoiled Matilda's ice cream. There was a trembling of other thoughts, too, around these, that were also rather unwelcome.

But she could not think them out then. The company had left the table and gathered in another room, and there a great deal of talk and discussion of many things went on, including winter plans for the children and home arrangements, in which Matilda was interested. Shopping, also, and what stuffs and what colours were most in favour, and fashions of making and wearing. Matilda had certainly been used to hear talk on such subjects in the days of her mother's life-time, when the like points were eagerly debated between her and her older children. But then it was always with questions. *What* is fashionable; and *What* can we manage to get? Now and here, that questioning was replaced by calm knowledge and certainty and the power to do as they pleased. So the subject became doubly interesting. The two boys had gone off together; and the two girls, mixing with the group of their elders, listened and formed their own opinions, of each other at least. For every now and then, the black eyes and the brown eyes met; glances inquiring, determining, but almost as nearly repellant as anything else. So passed the evening; and Matilda was very glad when it was time to go to bed.

Mrs. Laval went with her to her pretty room, and saw with motherly care that all was in order and everything there which ought to be there. The room was warm, though no fire was to be seen; the gas was lit; and complete luxury filled every corner and met every want, even of the eye. And after a fond good night, Matilda was left to herself. She was in a very confused state of mind. It was a strange place; she half wished they were back in Shadywalk; but with that were mixed floating visions of shopping and her filled wardrobe, visions of driving in the Park with Norton, fancies of untold wonderful things to be seen in this new great city, with its streets and its shops and its rich and its poor people. No, she could not forego the seeing of these; she was glad to be in New York; were there not the Menagerie and Stewart's awaiting her to-morrow? But what sort of a life she was to live here, and how far it would be possible for her to be like the Matilda Englefield of Shadywalk — why, she was *not* to be Matilda Englefield at all, but Laval. Could that be the same? Slowly, while she thought all this, Matilda opened her little trunk and took out her nightdress and her comb and brush, and her Bible; and then, the habit was as fixed as the other habit of going to bed, she opened her Bible, brought a pretty little table that was in the room, put it under the gas light, and knelt down to read and pray. She opened anywhere, and read without very well understanding what she read; the thoughts of lions and tigers, and green poplin, and red cashmere, making a strange web with the lines of Bible thought, over which her eye travelled. Till her eyes came to a word so plain, so clear, and touching her so nearly, that she all at once as it were woke up out of her maze.

"*Who mind earthly things.*"

What is that? Must one not mind earthly
things? Then she went back to the beginning of the sentence, to see better what it
meant.

" For many walk, of whom I have told you
often, and now tell you even weeping, that
they are the enemies of the cross of Christ:
whose end is destruction, whose God is their
belly, and whose glory is in their shame, who
mind earthly things."

Must one not *mind* earthly things? thought
Matilda. How can one help minding them?
How can I help it? All the people in this
house mind nothing else. Neither did they
all at home, when mother was alive, mind
anything else. Mr. Richmond does. —

She went back now to the beginning of the
chapter and read it anew. It was easier to
read than to think. The chapter was the
third of Philippians. She did not know who
wrote it; she did not exactly understand a
good part of it; nevertheless one thing was

clear, a heart set on something not earthly, and minding nothing that interfered with or did not help that. So much was clear; and also that the chapter spoke of certain people not moved by a like spirit, as enemies of the cross of Christ. It was the hardest reading, Matilda thought, she had ever done in her Bible. If this is what it is to be a Christian, it was easier to be a Christian when she was darning lace for Mrs. Candy and roasting coffee beans in her kitchen for Maria. But she did not wish to be back there. Some way could be found, surely, of being a Christian and keeping her pretty room and having her wardrobe filled. And here Matilda became so sleepy, the fatigue and excitement of this long day settling down upon her now that the day was over, that she could neither think nor read any more. She was obliged to go to bed.

CHAPTER VI.

THE second of December rose keen and clear, like the first; but inside Matilda's room there was a state of pleasant summer temperature; she could hardly understand that it was cold enough outside to make the pretty frosting on her window panes which hindered the view. She dressed in royal comfort, and in a delightful stir of expectation and hope. It was really New York; and she was going to Stewart's to-day. The cold would not bite her as it used to do in Shadywalk, for they would be in a carriage.

When she was dressed she contrived to clear a loophole in her frosted window, and looked out. The sun shone on a long, clean, handsome street, lined with houses that looked as if all New York were made of

money. Brick and stone fronts rose to
stately heights, as far as her eye could see;
windows were filled with beautiful large
panes of glass, like her own window, and lace
and drapery behind them testified to the inside adorning and beautifying. There could
not be any one living in all that street who
was not rich; nothing but plenty and ease
could possibly be behind such house-fronts.
Then Matilda saw an omnibus going down
the street; but her breath dimmed her look-
out place and she had to give it up for that
time. It was her hour for reading and praying. Matilda was a little inclined to shrink
from it, fearing lest she might come upon
some other passage that would give her
trouble. She thought, for this morning, she
would turn to a familiar chapter, which she
had read many a time, and where she had
never found anything to confuse her. She
began the fifth of Matthew. But she had read
only fifteen verses, and she came to this.

"Let your light so shine before men, that

they may see your good works, and glorify your Father which is in heaven."

If a ray of the very sunshine, pointed and tipped with fire like a spear, so that it could prick her, had come in through the frosting on the window pane and smote upon Matilda's face, she would not more keenly have felt the touch.   It had never touched her before, that verse, with anything but rose leaf softness; now it pricked.   Why?   The little girl was troubled; and leaning her elbows on the table and her head in her hands, she began to think.   And then she began to pray. "Let your light shine."   The light must burn if it was to shine; that was one thing; and she must let no screen come between the light and those who should see it.   Fear must not come there, nor shame, to hide or cover the light.   And the light itself must be bright.   Nobody would see a dim shining. By and by, as she pondered and prayed, with her head in her hands, this word and last night's word joined themselves together; and she began to see, that "minding earthly things" would act to hide the light first, and then to put it out. So far she got; but the battle was only set in array; it was not fought nor gained, when she was called down to breakfast.

The rest of the family were all seated at the table before the two boys came in.

"Pink," Norton burst forth, as soon as he had said good morning, "we must get there at feeding time!"

"Here you are!" — said David waggishly; and Matilda looking up, saw Judith's black eyes all on fire and a flash of the same fun in her brother's face. Those proud eyes could sparkle, then. Her look passed to Norton. But he was as cool as usual.

"Mamma," he said, "I am going to take Pink this morning to the Menagerie."

"You had better wait till she has something to wear, Norton."

"When will that be, ma'am? It won't take long will it?"

" I do not know."

" Mamma, Pink does not care, and I do not care. She has never seen a live lion in her life ; and it will not make any difference with the lions. I guess she will keep warm. I want to be there at twelve o'clock ; or I want to be there before. They feed the animals at twelve o'clock, and they're all alive."

" We feed the animals here at one o'clock," said his grandmother. " I hope you will remember that."

" Do you want to go, Matilda ? " Mrs. Laval asked.

" She has never seen a lion," repeated Norton.

" Somebody else has never seen a monkey," said Judith.

" That is somebody who don't live in the house with Judy Bartholomew," Norton returned.

" We don't want to see a bear, either," said Miss Judy pouting.

" Well, remember and be at home for luncheon," said Mrs. Laval. " I want Matilda after that."

The breakfast went on now delightfully. Matilda sometimes lifted her eyes to look at her opposite neighbours; they had a fascination for her. Judith was such a sprite of mischief, to judge from her looks; and David was so utterly unlike Norton. Norton was always acute and frank, outspoken when he had a mind, fearless and careless at all times. Fearless David might be, but not careless, unless his face belied him; he did not look as if it were often his pleasure to be outspoken, or to shew what he was thinking of. And that was the oddest of all, that he did not seem lighthearted. Matilda fancied he was proud; she was sure that he was reserved. In the family gatherings he was seen but not heard; and she thought he did not care much for what was going on. Nothing escaped Judy's ears or eyes; and nothing was serious with her which she could turn into fun. Her eyes gave a funny snap now and then when

12

they met Matilda's eyes across the table, as if she had her own thoughts about Matilda and knew half of Matilda's thoughts about her. Matilda hoped she would not take it into her head to go to the Menagerie.

" Norton, I believe I'll go too," said Judith the next minute.

" Where ? " said Norton.

" To the Menagerie. Where should I go ? "

" All right," said Norton. " But if you are going to do me the honour to go with me, you must wait till I have brought Matilda back. I can't take care of both of you."

" I don't want you to take care of me," said Judy.

" I know that. But I am going to take care of Matilda."

" Why cannot you take care of both of them ? " his grandmother asked, interrupting Judith.

" Make Judith tell first why she wants to

go, grandmamma. She has been lots of times."

"Grandmamma," said Judy with her eyes snapping, "I want to see a new sort of wild animal, just come, and to see how it will look at the tigers."

They all laughed, but Mrs. Laval put her arm round Matilda and stooped down and kissed her.

"Judith is a wild animal herself, isn't she, dear? She is a sort of little wild-cat. But she has soft paws; they don't scratch."

Matilda was not quite so sure of this. However, when they left the table Judith set about gaining her point in earnest; but Norton was not to be won over. He was going with Matilda alone, he said, the first time; and so he did.

It was all enjoyment then, as soon as Matilda and Norton left the house together. Matilda was in a new world. Her eyes were busy making observations everywhere.

"How beautiful the houses are, Norton,"

she said, when they had gone a block or two. " There are not many poor people in New York, are there ? "

" Well, occasionally you see one," said Norton.

" I don't see anything that looks like one. Norton, why do they have the middle of the street covered with those round stones ? They make such a racket when the carts and carriages go over them. It is very disagreeable."

" Is it ? " said Norton. " You won't hear it after you have been here a little while."

" Not hear it? But why do they have it so, Norton ? "

" Why Pink, just think of the dust we should have, and the mud, if it was all like Shadywalk, and these thousands of wheels cutting into it all the time."

Matilda was silenced. One difference brings on another, she was learning to find out. But now Norton hailed a street car and they got into it. The warmth of the car was very pleasant after the keen wind in the streets. And here also the people who filled it, though most of them certainly not rich people, and many very far from that, yet looked to a certain degree comfortable. But just as Norton and Matilda got out, and were about to enter the building, where an enormous painted canvass with a large brown lion upon it told that the Menagerie was to be seen, Matilda stopped short. A little ragged boy, about as old as herself, offered her a handful of black round-headed pins. What did he mean? Matilda looked at him, and at the pins.

"Come on," cried Norton. " What is that? — No, we don't want any of your goods just now; at least I don't. Come in, Pink. You need not stop to speak to everybody that stops to speak to you."

" What did he want, Norton? that boy."

" Wanted to sell hairpins. Didn't you see?"

Matilda cast a look back at the sideway,

where the boy was trying another passenger for custom; but Norton drew her on, and the boy was forgotten in some extraordinary noises she heard; she had heard them as soon as she entered the door; strange, mingled noises, going up and down a scale of somewhat powerful, unearthly notes. She asked Norton what they were?

"The lions, Pink," said Norton, with intense satisfaction. "The lions, and the rest of the company. Come — here they are."

And having paid his fee, he pushed open a swinging baize door, and they entered a very long room or gallery, where the sounds became to be sure very unmistakable. They almost terrified Matilda. So wildly were mingled growls and cries and low roarings, all in one restless, confused murmur. The next minute she all but forgot the noise. She was looking at two superb Bengal tigers, a male and a female, in one large cage. They were truly superb. Large and lithe, magnificent in port and action, beautiful in the colour and marking of their smooth hides. But restless ? That is no word strong enough to fit the ceaseless impatient movement with which the male tiger went from one corner of his iron cage to the other corner, and back again; changing constantly only to renew the change. One bound in his native jungle would have carried him over many times the space, which now he paced eagerly or angrily with a few confined steps. The tigress meanwhile knew his mood and her wisdom so well that she took care never to be in his way; and as the cage was not large enough to allow her mate to turn round in the corner where she stood, she regularly took a flying leap over his back whenever he came near that corner. Again and again and again, the one lordly creature trod from end to end the floor of his prison; and every time, like a feather, so lightly and gracefully, the huge powerful form of the other floated over his back and alighted in the other corner.

"Do they keep doing that all the time!"

said Matilda, when she had stood spell-bound before the cage for some minutes.

" It's near feeding time," said Norton. " I suppose they know it and it makes them worry. Or else know they are hungry; which answers just as well."

" Poor creatures!" said Matilda. " If that tiger could break his cage, now, how far do you think he could jump, Norton?"

" I don't know," said Norton. " As far as to you or me, I guess. Or else over all our heads, to get at that coloured woman."

The woman was sweeping the floor, a little way behind the two talkers, and heard them. " Yes!" she said, " he'd want me fust thing, sure."

" Why?" whispered Matilda.

" Likes the dark meat best," said Norton. " Fact, Pink; they say they do."

Matilda gazed with a new fascination on the beautiful, terrible creatures. Could it be possible, that those very animals had actually tasted " dark meat " at home?

" Yes," said Norton; "there are hundreds of the natives carried off and eaten by the tigers, I heard a gentleman telling mother, every year, in the province of Bengal alone. Come, Pink ; we can look at these fellows again ; I want you to see some of the others before they are fed."

They went on, with less delay, till they came to the Russian bear. At the great blocks of ice in his cage Matilda marvelled.

" Is he so warm ! " she said. " In this weather ? "

" This room's pretty comfortable," said Norton; " and to him I suppose it's as bad as a hundred and fifty degrees of the thermometer would be to us. He's accustomed to fifty degrees below zero."

" I don't know what ' below zero ' means, exactly," said Matilda. " But then those great pieces of ice cannot do him much good?"

" Not much," said Norton.

" And he must be miserable," said Matilda; "just that we may look at him."

" Do you wish he was back again where he came from?" said Norton; "all comfortable, with ice at his back and ice under his feet; where we couldn't see him?"

" But Norton, isn't it cruel ? "

" Isn't what cruel ? "

" To have him here, just for our pleasure ? I am very glad to see him, of course."

" I thought you were," said Norton. " Why I suppose we cannot have anything, Pink, without somebody being uncomfortable for it, somewhere. I am very often uncomfortable myself."

Matilda was inclined to laugh at him; but there was no time. She had come face to face with the lions. Except for those low strange roars, they did not impress her as much as their neighbours from Bengal. But she studied them, carefully enough to please Norton, who was making a very delight to himself, and a great study, of her pleasure.

Further on, Matilda was brought to a long

stand again before the wolf's cage. It was a small cage, so small that in turning round he rubbed his nose against the wall at each end; for the ends were boarded up; and the creature did nothing but turn round. At each end of the cage there was a regular spot on the boards, made by his nose as he lifted it a little to get round the more easily, and yet not enough to avoid touching. Yet he went round and round, restlessly, without stopping for more than an instant at a time.

"Poor fellow, poor fellow!" was again Matilda's outcry. "He keeps doing that all the time, Norton; see the places where his nose rubs."

"Don't say 'poor fellow' about a wolf," said Norton.

"Why not? He is only an animal."

"He is a wicked animal."

"Why Norton, he don't know any better than to be wicked. Do you think some animals are really worse than others?"

"I'm certain of it," said Norton.

" But they only do what it is their nature to do."

" Yes, and different animals have different natures. Now look at that wolf's eyes; see what cruel, sly, bad eyes they are. Think what beautiful eyes a horse has; a good horse."

" And sheep have beautiful eyes," said Matilda.

" And pigs have little, ugly, dirty eyes; mean and wicked too. You need not laugh; it is true."

" I don't know how pigs' eyes look," said Matilda. " But it is very curious. For of course *they* do not know any better; so how should they be wicked? Those tigers, they looked as if they hadn't any heart at all. Don't you think a dog has a heart, Norton ? "

Norton laughed, and pulled her on to a cage at a little distance from the wolf, where there were a party of monkeys. And next door to them was a small ape in a cell alone.

Matilda forgot everything else here. These creatures were so inimitably odd, sly and comical; had such an air of knowing what they were about, and expecting you to understand it too; looking at you as though they could take you into their confidence, if it were worth while; it was impossible to get away from them. Norton had some nuts in his pocket; with these he and the monkeys made great game; while the little ape raked in the straw litter of his cage to find any stray seeds or bits of food which might have sifted down through it to the floor, managing his long hand-like paw as gracefully as the most elegant lady could move her dainty fingers. Matilda and Norton staid with the monkeys, till the feeding hour had arrived; then Norton hurried back to the tigers. A man was coming the rounds with a basket full of great joints of raw meat; and it was notable to see how carefully he had to manage to let the tiger have his piece before the tigress got hers. He watched and waited, till he got a chance to thrust the meat into the cage at the end where the tiger's paw would the next instant be.

" Why ? " Matilda asked Norton.

" There'd be an awful fight, I guess, if he didn't," said Norton; " and that other creature would stand a chance to get whipped; and her coat would be scratched; that's all the man cares for."

" And is that the reason the tigress keeps out of the tiger's way so ? "

" Of course. Some people would say, I suppose, that she was *amiable*."

" I never should, to look in her face," said Matilda laughing. " Tigers certainly are wicked. But, they do not know any better. How can it be wickedness ? "

" Now come, Pink," said Norton; " we have got to be home by one, you know, and there's a fellow you haven't seen yet; the hippopotamus. We must go into another place to see him."

He was by himself, in a separate room, as

Norton had said, where a large tank was prepared and filled with water for his accommodation. Matilda looked at him a long time in silence and with great attention.

" Do you know, Norton," she said, " this is the *behemoth* the Bible speaks about? "

" I don't know at all," said Norton. " How do you know ? "

" Mr. Richmond says so ; he says people have found out that it is so. But he don't seem to me very big, Norton, for that."

The keeper explained, that the animal was a young one and but half grown.

" How tremendously ugly he is ! " said Norton.

" And what a wonderful number of different animals there are in the world," said Matilda. " This is unlike anything I ever saw. I wonder why there are such a number ? "

" And so many of them not good for anything," said Norton.

" Oh Norton, you can't say that, you know."

" Why not? This fellow, for instance; what is he good for?"

" I don't know; and you don't know. But that's just it, Norton. You *don't* know."

" Well, what are lions and tigers good for?" said Norton. " I suppose we know about them. What are they good for?"

" Why Norton, I can't tell," said Matilda. " I would very much like to know. But they must be good for something."

" To eat up people, and make the places where they live a terror," said Norton.

" I don't know," said Matilda, with a very puzzled look on her little face. " It seems so strange, when you think of it. And those great serpents, Norton, that live where the lions and tigers live; they are worse yet."

" Little and big," said Norton. " I do despise a snake!"

" And crocodiles," said Matilda. " And wolves, and bears. I wonder if the Bible tells anything about it."

" The Bible don't tell everything, Pink,"
said Norton laughing.

" No, but I remember now what it *does*
say," said Matilda. " It says that God saw
everything that he had made, and it was very
good."

Norton looked with a funny look at his
little companion, amused and yet with a
kind of admiration mixed with his amusement.

" I wonder how you and David would get
along," he remarked. " He is as touchy on
that subject as you are."

" What subject ? " said Matilda. " The
Bible ? "

" The Old Testament. The Jewish Script-
ures. Not the New ! Don't ever bring up
the *New* Testament to him, Pink, unless you
want stormy weather."

" Is he bad-tempered ? " Matilda asked
curiously.

" He's Jewish-tempered," said Norton.
" He has his own way of looking at things,

13

and he don't like yours. I mean, anybody's but his own. What a quantity it must take to feed this enormous creature!"

" You may take your affidavit of that!" said the keeper, who was an Irishman. " Faith, I think he's as bad as fifty men."

" What do you give him ? "

" Well, he belongs to the vegetable kingdom intirely, ye see, sir."

" He's a curious water-lily, isn't he ? " said Norton low to Matilda. But that was more than either of them could stand, and they turned away and left the place to laugh. It was time then, they found, to go home.

A car was not immediately in sight when they came out into the street, and Norton and Matilda walked a few blocks rather than stand still. It had grown to be a very disagreeable day. The weather was excessively cold, and a very strong wind had risen; which now went careering along the streets, catching up all the dust of them in turn, and before letting it drop again whirling it furiously against everybody in its way. Matilda struggled along, but the dust came in thick clouds and filled her eyes and mouth and nose and lodged in all her garments. It seemed to go through everything she had on, and with the dirt came the cold. Shadywalk never saw anything like this! As they were crossing one of the streets in their way, Matilda stopped short just before setting her foot on the curb-stone. A little girl with a broom in her hand stood before her and held out her other hand for a penny. The child was ragged, and her rags were of the colour of the dust which filled everything that day; hair and face and dress were all of one hue.

" Please, a penny," she said, barring Matilda's way.

" Norton, have you got a penny?" said Matilda bewildered.

" Nonsense!" said Norton, "we can't be bothered to stop for all the street-sweepers

we meet. Come on, Pink." He seized
Matilda's hand, and she was drawn on, out
of the little girl's range, before she could stop
to think about it. Two streets further on,
they crossed an avenue; and here Matilda
saw two more children with brooms, a boy
and a girl. This time she saw what they
were about. They were sweeping the crossing clean for the feet of the passers-by. But
their own feet were bare on the stones. The
next minute Norton had hailed a car and he
and Matilda got in. Her eyes and mouth
were so full of dust and she was so cold, it
was a little while before she could ask questions comfortably.

"What are those children you wouldn't
let me speak to?" she said, as soon as she
was a little recovered.

"Street-sweepers," said Norton. "Regular
nuisances! The police ought to take them
up, and shut them up."

"Why, Norton?"

"Why? why because they're such a nui-

sance. You can't walk a half mile without having half a dozen of them holding out their hands for pennies. A fellow can't carry his pocket full of pennies and keep it full!"

"But they sweep the streets, don't they?"

"The crossings; yes. I wish they didn't. They are an everlasting bother."

"But Norton, isn't it nice to have the crossings swept? I thought it was a great deal pleasanter than to have to go through the thick dust and dirt which was everywhere else."

"Yes, but when they come every block or two?" said Norton.

"Are there so many of them?"

"There's no end to them," said Norton.

"But at any rate, there are just as many crossings," said Matilda. "And they must be either dirty or clean."

"I can get along with the crossings," said Norton.

" Well, your boots are thick. Haven't those children any way to get a living but *such* a way ? "

" Of course not, or they wouldn't do that, I suppose."

" But their feet were *bare*, Norton; they were *bare*, on those cold dirty stones."

" Dirt is nothing," said Norton, buttoning up his great coat comfortably. He had just loosened it to get at some change for the car fare.

" Dirt is nothing ? " repeated Matilda looking at him.

" I mean, Pink," said he laughing, " it is nothing to them. They are as dirty as they can be already; a little more or less makes no difference."

" I wonder if they are as cold as they can be, too," said Matilda meditatively.

" No ! " said Norton. " Not they. They are used to it. They don't feel it."

" How can you tell, Norton ? "

" I can tell. I can see. They are jolly

enough sometimes; when they aren't boring for cents."

"But that little girl, Norton, — all of them, — they hadn't much on!"

"No," said Norton; "I suppose not. It's no use to look and think about it, Pink. They are accustomed to it; it isn't what it would be to you. Don't think about it. You'll be always seeing sights in New York. The best way is *not* to see."

But Matilda did think about it. "Not what it would be to her"! why, it would kill *her*, very quickly. Of course it must be not exactly so to these children, since they did not die; but what was it to them? Not warmth and comfort; not a pleasant spending of time for pleasure.

"Norton," she began again just as they were getting out of the car, "it seems to me that if those children sweep the streets, it is right to give them pay for it. They are trying to earn something."

"You can't," said Norton. "There are too

many of them. You cannot be putting your hand in your pocket for pennies all the while, and stopping under the heels of the horses. I do once in a while give them something. You can't be doing it always."

CHAPTER VII.

NORTON asked to be allowed to go with the shopping party, which his mother refused. To Matilda's disappointment, she took Miss Judy instead. Matilda would rather have had any other one of the household. However, nothing could spoil the pleasure of driving to Stewart's. To know it so cold, and yet feel so comfortable; to see how the dust flew in whirlwinds and the wind caught people and staggered them, and yet not to be touched by a breath; to see how the foot travellers had to fight with both wind and dust, and to feel at the same time the easy security, the safe remove from everything so ugly and disagreeable, which they themselves enjoyed behind the glass of their Clarence; it was a very pleasant experience.

The other two did not seem to enjoy it; they were accustomed to the sensation, or it had ceased to be one for them. Matilda was in a state of delight every foot of the way. *This* was what she had come to, this safety and ease and elegance and immunity. She was higher than the street or the street-goers, by just so much as the height of the axletree of the carriage. How about those little dust covered street-sweepers?

The thought of them jarred. There was nothing between *them* and the roughest of the rough. How came they to be there, at the street corners, and Matilda here, behind these clear plates of glass which enclosed the front of the carriage?

"How very disagreeable it is to day!" Mrs. Laval said with a shudder. "This is some of New York's worst weather."

"It's just horrid!" said Judy.

"I would not take a walk to-day, for all I am worth," the lady went on. "There is one thing; there will be fewer people out, and we shall not have to wait so fearfully long to be served."

The carriage stopped before a large white building, and Matilda followed the others in, full of curiosity and eager pleasure. In through the swinging doors, and then through such a crowd of confusion that she could think of nothing but to keep close behind Mrs. Laval; till they all stopped at a counter and Mrs. Laval sat down. What a wonderful place it seemed to Matilda! A small world that was all shops — or one shop; and the only business of that world was buying and selling things to wear. Just at this counter people were getting silk dresses, it appeared; here, and all round the room in which Mrs. Laval was seated; blue and rose silks were displayed in one part; black silks before some customers; figured and parti-coloured silks were held up to please others; what colour was there not? and what beauty? Matilda found that whatever Mrs. Laval wanted of her that afternoon, it was not any help in making her purchases; and she was quite at liberty to use her eyes upon everything. The beautiful goods on the counters were the great attraction, however; Matilda could not look away much from the lustre of the crimson and green and blue and tawny and grey and lavender which were successively or together exhibited for Mrs. Laval's behoof; and she listened to find out if she could by the quantities ordered, which of them, if any, were for herself. She was pretty sure that a dark green and a crimson had that destination; and her little heart beat high with pleasure.

From the silk room they went on to another where the articles were not interesting to look at; and Matilda discovered that the coming and going people *were.* She turned her back upon the counter and watched the stream as it flowed past and around her. Miss Judith also here found herself thrown out of amusement, and came round to Matilda. They had hardly spoken to each other hitherto. Now Miss Judy's eye first went up and down the little figure which was such a new one in her surroundings. Matilda knew it, but she could bear it.

" You were never here before ? " said her companion.

" Never," Matilda answered.

" What do you think of it ? "

" I think they have nice things here," said Matilda.

Judith did not at all know what to make of this answer.

" What is aunt Zara going to get for you ? "

" I do not know — some dresses, I think."

Judith's eye ran up and down Matilda's dress again. " That was made in the country, wasn't it ? "

" Mrs. Laval had it made."

" Yes, but you will want another. Aunt Zara — aunt Zara ! — Aren't you going to get her a cloak ? "

" A cloak ? " said Mrs. Laval looking

round. "Yes; that is what I brought her for."

"There!" said Judy, "now you know something you didn't know before. What sort of a cloak would you like?"

"I don't know," said Matilda in a flutter of delight. "Mrs. Laval knows."

"I suppose she does, but she doesn't know what you would like, unless you tell her. Let us watch the people coming in and see if we see anything you would like. Isn't it funny?"

"What?" Matilda asked.

"All of it. To see the people. They are all sorts, you know, and so funny. There are two Irish women, — very likely they have come in from the shanties near the Central Park, to buy some calico dresses. Look at them! — ten cent calicoes, and they are asking the shopman, I dare say, if they can't have that one for nine. I suppose the calicoes are made for them. No, there is somebody else wanting one. She's from the country."

" How do you know ? "

" Easy enough. See how she has got her hands folded over each other; nobody does that but somebody that has come from the country. See her hat, too; that's a country hat. If you could see her feet, you would see that she has great thick country shoes."

Judy's eye as she spoke glanced down again at the floor where Matilda's feet stood; and it seemed to Matilda that the very leather of her boots could feel the look. *They* were country boots. Did Judy mean that?

" There's another country woman," the young lady went on. " See? — this one in a velvet cloak. That's a cotton velvet, though."

" But how can you tell she's from the country ? "

" She's all corners! " said Judith. " Her cloak was made by a carpenter, and her head looks as if it was made by a mason. If you could see her open her mouth, I've no doubt you would find that it is square. There! —

here! — how would you like a cloak like this
one ?"

The two were looking at a child who
passed them just then, in a velvet cloak stiff
with gimp and bugle embroidery.

" I don't think it is pretty," said Matilda.

" It is rich," said Judy. " But it is not
cut by anybody that knew how. You can
see that. Why don't you ask aunt Zara to
let you have a black satin cloak ?"

" Black satin ?" said Matilda.

" Yes. Black satin. It is so rich; and it
is not heavy; and there is more shine to it
than silk has. A black satin cloak trimmed
with velvet — that is what I should like if I
were you."

A strong desire for a black satin cloak
forthwith sprang up in Matilda's mind.

" There is not anything more fashionable,"
Judy went on; " and velvet is just the pret-
tiest trimming. When we go up to look at
cloaks, you see if you can spy such a one; if
you can't, it would be easy to get the stuff

and have it made. Just as easy. I don't
believe we shall find any ready made, for
they are so fashionable, they will be likely to
be all bought up. Dear me! what a figure
that is!" exclaimed Judy, eying a richly
dressed lady who brushed by them.

"Isn't her dress handsome?" Matilda
asked.

"It was handsome before it was made up
—it isn't now. Dresses are not cut that
way now; and the trimming is as old as the
hills. I guess that has been made two or
three years, that dress. And nobody wears
a shawl now—unless it's a camel's hair.
Nobody would, that knew any better."

"What is a camel's hair?" said Matilda.

"A peculiar sort of rough thick shawl,"
said Judy. "People wear them because they
set off the rest of their dress; but country
people don't know enough to wear them.
Ask aunt Zara to get you a camel's hair
shawl. I wish she would give me one, too."

Matilda wondered why Miss Judith's

14

mother did not get her one, if they were
so desirable; but she did not feel at home
enough with the young lady to venture any
such suggestion.   She only did wish very
much privately that Mrs. Laval would choose
for herself a black satin cloak; but on that
score too she did not feel that she could
make any requests.   Mrs. Laval knew what
was fashionable, at any rate, as well as her
niece; that was one comfort.

Thinking this, Matilda followed her two
companions up the wide staircase.   Another
world of shops and buyers and sellers up
there!   What a very wonderful place New
York must be.   And Stewart's.

"Does everybody come here?" she whispered to Judy.

"Pretty much everybody," said that young
lady.   "They have to."

"Then they can't buy things anywhere
else?"

"What do you mean?" said Judith looking at her.

" I mean, is this the only place where people can get things? are there any more stores beside this?"

Judith's eyes snapped in a way that Matilda resolved she would not provoke again.

" More stores?" she said. " New York is *all* stores, except the streets where people live."

" Does nobody live in the streets where the stores are?" Matilda could not help asking.

" No. Nobody but the people that live *in* the stores, you know; that's nobody."

Matilda's thoughts were getting rather confused than enlightened; however the party came now, passing by a great variety of counters and goods displayed, to a region where Matilda saw there was a small host of cloaks, hung upon frames' or stuffed figures. Here Mrs. Laval sat down on a sofa and made Matilda sit down, and called for something that would suit the child's age and size. Velvet, and silk and cloth, and shaggy nondescript stuffs, were in turn brought for-

ward; Matilda saw no satin. Mrs. Laval
was hard to suit; and Matilda thought Judith was no help, for she constantly put in a
word for the articles which Mrs. Laval dis-
approved. Matilda was not consulted at
all, and indeed neither was Miss Judy. At
last a cloak was chosen, not satin, nor even
silk, nor even cloth; but of one of those
same shaggy fabrics which looked coarse,
Matilda thought. But she noticed that the
price was not low, and that consoled her.
The cloak was taken down to the carriage,
and they left the store.

"Where now, aunt Zara?" said Judith.
"We are pretty well lumbered up with packages."

"To get rid of some of them," said Mrs.
Laval. "I am going to Fournissons's."

What that meant, Matilda could not guess.
The drive was somewhat long; and then the
carriage stopped before a plain-looking house
in a very plain-looking street. Here they all
got out again, and taking the various parcels

which contained Matilda's dresses, they went
in. They mounted to a common little sit-
ting-room, where some litter was strewn
about on the floor. But a personage met
them there for whom Matilda very soon con-
ceived a high respect; she knew so much.
This was Mme. Fournissons; the mantua-
maker who had the pleasure of receiving
Mrs. Laval's orders. So she said; but Matilda thought the orders rather came from
the other side. Mme. Fournissons decided
promptly how everything ought to be made,
and just what trimming would be proper in
each case; and proceeded to take Matilda's
measure with a thorough-bred air of knowing
her business which impressed Matilda very
much. Tapes unrolled themselves deftly,
and pins went infallibly into place and never
out of place; and Madame measured and
fitted and talked all at once, with the smooth
rapid working of a first-rate steam engine.
New York mantua-making was very different
from the same thing at Shadywalk! And

here Matilda saw the wealth of her new wardrobe unrolled. There was a blue merino and a red cashmere and a brown rep, for daily wear; and there was a most beautiful crimson silk and a dark green one for other occasions. There was a blue crape also, with which Miss Judy evidently fell in love.

" It would not become you, Judy, with your black eyes," her aunt said. " Now Matilda is fair; it will suit her."

" Charmingly!" Mme. Fournissons had added. " Just the thing. There is a delicacy of skin which will set off the blue, and which the blue will set off. Miss Bartholomew should wear the colours of the dahlia — as her mother knows."

" Clear straw colour, for instance, and purple!" said Judith scornfully.

" Mrs. Bartholomew has not such bad taste," said Mme. Fournissons. " This is ? — this young lady ?" —

" My adopted daughter, madame," said Mrs. Laval.

" She will not dishonour your style, madam," rejoined the mantua-maker approvingly."

Judith pouted. She could do that well. But Matilda went down the stairs happy. Now she was sure her dress would be quite as handsome and quite as fashionable as Judy's; there would be no room for glances of depreciation, or such shrugs of disdain as had been visited upon the country people coming to Stewart's. All would be strictly correct in her attire, and according to the latest and best mode. The wind blew as hard as ever, and the dust swept in furious charges against everybody in the street by turns; but there were folds of silk and velvet, as well as sheets of plate glass now, between Matilda and it. When they reached home, Mrs. Laval called Matilda into her room.

" Here are your five dollars for December, my darling," she said. " Have you any boots beside those ? "

" No, ma'am."

" You want another pair of boots; and
then you will do very well until next month.
Norton can take you to the shoemaker's to-
morrow, — he likes to take you everywhere;
tell him it must be Laddler's.   And you will
want to go and see your sisters, will you
not ? "

" O yes, ma'am."

" Where is it ? "

Matilda named the place.

"316 Bolivar St.," repeated Mrs. Laval.
" Bolivar St. Where is that ? Bolivar
Street is away over on the other side of the
city, I think, towards what they used to call
Chelsea.   You could not possibly walk there.
I will let the carriage take you.   Now darling,
get ready for dinner."

Feeling as if she were ten years older than
she had been the day before, Matilda mounted
the stairs to her room. *Her* room. This
beautiful, comfortable, luxurious place !   It
was a little hard to recognize herself in it.
And when all those dresses should come
home —

Here there was a knock at the door, and Sam, the head waiter, handed her the bundle of her new cloak, in a nice pasteboard box. Matilda put that in the wardrobe drawer, and made her hair and dress neat; not without a dim notion, back somewhere in her heart, that she had a good deal of thinking to do. A feeling that she was somehow getting out of her reckoning. There was no time however now for anything before the bell rang for dinner.

Nor all the evening. Norton was eager with questions; and Judith was sharp with funny speeches, about Matilda's wonder and unusedness to everything. Matilda winced a little; however, Norton laughed it off, and the evening on the whole went pleasantly. He and she arranged schemes for to-morrow; and all the four got a little more acquainted with each other. But when Matilda went up to her room at night, she took out her Bible and opened it, resolving to find out what those things were she had to think of; she seemed to have switched off her old track and to have got a great way from Mr. Richmond and Shadywalk. She did not like this feeling. What did it mean?

She tried to think, but she could not think. Folds of glossy blue silk hung before her eyes; her new odd little cloak, with its rich buttons and tassels started up to her vision; Mme. Fournissons and her tape measure and her face and her words came putting themselves between her and the very words of the Bible. And this went on. What was she to do? Matilda sat back from the table and tried to call herself to order. *This* was not the way to do. And then her mind flew off to the Menagerie, and the roars of those wild beasts seemed to go up and down in her ears. Yet underneath all these things, there was a secret consciousness of something not right; *was* it there, or no? It was all a whirl of confusion. Matilda tried to recollect Mr. Richmond and some of his words.

"He said I was to go by that motto,

' Whatsoever ye do, in word or deed, do all'
— Well, but I am not doing anything, am
I, just now? What have I been doing to-
day? I will take a piece of paper and put
the things down! and then my thoughts will
not slip away so."

Matilda got the piece of paper and the pen-
cil; but she did not immediately find out
what she was to put down.

" The Menagerie ? — I did not go there of
my own head; Norton took me. Still,
'*whatsoever* ye do' — I was getting pleasure, that's all; it was nothing but pleasure.
What has my motto to do with pleasure?
Well, of course it would make it impossible
for me to take wrong pleasure — I see that.
I could not take pleasure that would be wrong
in God's sight, nor that would make me do
wrong to get it. Other pleasure, right pleasure, he likes me to have. Yes, and he gives
it to me, really. I couldn't have it else.
Then certainly my motto says that I must
remember that, and thank Him first of all for

everything I have that I like. Did I do so about the Menagerie? I don't think I thought about it at all; only I was very much obliged to Norton. I did not thank God. And yet it was such a very, very great pleasure! But I will now."

And so Matilda did. Before going any further in her inquiries, she kneeled down and gave thanks for the rare enjoyment of the morning. She rose up a little more sober-minded and able for the other work on hand.

" What next? Those little street sweep-ers. I did not have anything to do with them — I had no pennies in my pocket, and I could not wait. But I shall be seeing them every day; they are under foot everywhere, Norton says; how ought I to behave towards them? They are a great nuisance, Norton says; stopping one at every corner; and they ought not to be encouraged. If nobody gave them anything, of course they would not be encouraged; and they would not be there sweeping the crossings. But then, we should not have clean crossings. I wonder which is worst, having them swept or not having them swept? However, they will be on the streets, I suppose, those poor children, whatever *I* do. Now what ought I to do? I can't give pennies to them all; and if not, how shall I manage?"

Matilda put her head down to think. And then came floating into her thoughts the words of her motto, — "Do all in the name of the Lord Jesus."

"What would He say?" questioned Matilda with herself. "But I know what he did say! 'Give to him that asketh thee.' — Must I? But how *can* I, to all these children? I shall not have pennies. Well, of course! when I *haven't* pennies I cannot give them. But I cannot buy candy much, then, can I! because I shall want all my odd cents. After all, they are working hard to get a living; how terribly hard it must be, to live so dirty and so cold! — and I have cake and ice cream and plenty of everything I like. I suppose I can do without candy. I know what Jesus would do too, if he was here; he would give them kind looks and kind words, as well as pay. But can I? What could I say to them? I wonder if Mrs. Laval would like me to speak to them? Anyhow, I *know* Jesus would say kind words to them — because He would love them. If I loved them, I could speak, easy enough. And then — He would try to do them good, and make them good. I wonder if they go to Sunday school, any of them? But I don't go myself yet, here. I suppose I shall " —

Matilda's wits went off on a long chase here, about things that had nothing to do with her piece of paper. At last came back.

" Where was I? what next? The next thing was the shopping. I had nothing to do with that. I did not ask for anything; it was all chosen and done without me. But this was another pleasure; and I am to take my dresses, and wear them of course, according to my motto. How can I? 'Do all in His name?' How can I? Well, to be sure, I can do it in such a way as to please him. How would that be?"

There seemed to be a great deal of confusion in Matilda's thoughts at this point, and hard to disentangle; but through it all she presently felt something like little soft blows of a hammer at her heart, reminding her of a very eager wish for black satin, and disappointment at not having it; of a violent desire to be fashionable, and to escape being thought unfashionable; and of a secret delight in rivalling Judith Bartholomew. And though Matilda tried to reason these thoughts away and explain them down, those soft blows of the hammer kept on, just as fast as ever.

"Does the Lord like such feelings? Does *he* care that his children should be fashionable? How are you going to dress to please him, if the object is to be as fine as Judith Bartholomew, or to escape her criticism, or to shew yourself a fine lady? Will that be pleasing him?"

The answer was swift to come; yet what was Matilda to do? All these things were at work in her already. And with them came now an ugly wicked wish, that religion did not require her to be unlike other people. But Matilda knew that was wicked, as soon as she felt it; and it humbled her. And what was she to do? Seeing the wrong of all these various feelings did not at all take them out of her heart. She *did* want to be fashionable; she was very glad to be as handsomely dressed as Judith; her heart was very much set on her silks and trimmings, in a way that conscience whispered was simply selfish and proud. Were these things going to change Matilda at once and make her a different child from the one that had been baptized in a black dress at Shadywalk, and only cared then for the "white robes" that are the spirit's adornings?

Matilda was determined that should not be.

She prayed a great deal about it; and at last went to bed, comforting herself with the assurance that the Lord would certainly help a child that trusted him, to be all that he had bidden her be.

The subject started itself anew the next morning; for there on her dressing-table lay her pocket book with the five dollars Mrs. Laval had given her last evening. There were two dollars also that were left from November's five dollars; that made seven, to go shopping for boots. " I should think I could do with that," Matilda thought to herself.

She asked Norton to go with her to Laddler's shoe store.

" Well," said Norton ; " but we must go to the Park to-day."

" And Madame Fournissons wants to see you this afternoon," said Mrs. Laval. " I think the Park must wait, Norton."

" But I have only to-day and to-morrow, mamma. School begins Monday."

" To-morrow will do for the Park," said

15

Mrs. Laval. "And you will have other Saturdays, Norton."

Matilda went upstairs to get ready, thinking that she was beginning to find out what sort of "opportunities" were likely to be given her in her new home. She was going to have opportunity for self-conquest, for self-denial, harder than she had ever known hitherto; opportunity to follow the straight path where it was not always easy to see it, and where it could only be found by keeping the face steadily in the right direction. In the midst of these thoughts, however, she dressed herself with great glee; put her purse in her pocket; and set out with Norton, remembering that in this matter of buying her boots her motto must come in play.

As it was rather early in the morning, the shoe store of Mr. Laddler was nearly empty, and Matilda had immediate attention. Matilda told what she wanted; the shopman glanced an experienced eye over her little figure, from her hat to the ground; gave her a seat, and proceeded to fit her. The very first pair of boots "went on like a glove," the man said. And they were very handsome. But the price was seven dollars! It would take her whole stock in hand.

" Can't you give me a pair that will cost less?" Matilda asked, after a pause of inward dismay.

" Those are what you want," said the man. " They fit, to a T; you cannot better that fit."

" But you have some that don't cost so much?"

" They would not look so well," said the shopman. " We have boots not finished in the same style, for less money; but you want those. That's the article."

" Please let me see the others."

He brought some to shew. They were of less fine and beautifully dressed stuff, were more coarsely made, and less elegant in their cut. Matilda saw all that, and hesitated. The man looked at her.

" There's a pair here," he said, turning back to his drawer, "that I can let you have for five dollars; — just as good as that first pair."

He produced them and tried one on. It seemed to be quite as he had said. Matilda could see no difference.

" That will do," said he, " if you like them. They are exactly as well made as that first pair; and of the same leather."

" Then why are they only five dollars," Matilda asked, " while the others are seven ? "

" Fashion," said the man. " Nothing else. You see, those are wide at the toe; that was the style worn last winter; these first, you see, are very narrow at the toe. There is no demand for *these* now; so I can let you have them low. If you like these, I will let you have them for four and a half. Seven dollar boots."

Matilda felt a pang of uncertainty. That would save her two and a half dollars of her seven, and she would have pennies for street girls and change for other objects. But Judy would look at those square toes, and think that Matilda was from the country and did not know, as she said, what was what. The thought of Judy's eyes and smile was not to be borne.

" I will take the others," she said hastily to the shopman — " the first you tried on."

" I thought so," said the man. " Those are what you want."

Matilda paid, and Norton ordered them sent home, and the two left the shop.

" If that had been a good shoemaker," said Norton, " he would have fitted you in half the time. We have been half an hour there."

" O that is my fault, Norton," said Matilda; "because I could not decide which fashion to have."

" Sure you have got the right one now?" said Norton.

" I got the newest."

" That's the right one," said Norton, as if the question was settled.

But it was not settled, in Matilda's mind;

and all the way home she was trying the boots over again. Had she done right? It was on her lips to say she wished there were no such thing as fashion, but conscience checked her; she felt it was very delightful to be *in the fashion.* Was that wrong? How could it be wrong? But she had paid for being in the fashion. Had she paid too much? And was she any the better for having round toes to her boots, that she should be so delighted about it? She wanted to be as well dressed as Judy. She wanted that Judy should not be able to laugh at her for a country girl. She could not help feeling that, she thought; but then, she had paid for it. Was this going to be the way always?

Matilda was in such a confusion of thoughts that she did not know what she was passing in the street. Only, she did know when there were little street-sweepers at the crossings, and she tried to slip by without seeming to see them, and to put Norton between them and herself. Not a penny had she for one of them. And she would not have, until the month came round again. Fashion certainly cost. But she had the narrow-toed boots; she was glad of that.

"What ails you?" said Norton at last. "Are you cold?"

"No, Norton. Nothing ails me. I am thinking."

"About what? You think a great deal too much. Pink, we will go to the Park this afternoon; that will give you something to think about."

"Norton, we cannot this afternoon, you know. I have got to go to the dressmaker's."

"O so you have! What a nuisance. Well, to-morrow, then. And I say, Pink! there is another thing you have to think of — Christmas presents."

"Christmas presents!" said Matilda.

"Yes; we always have a great time. Only David and Judy do scowl; it is fun to see them."

" Don't they like Christmas presents ? " said
Matilda, very much bewildered.

" Christmas *presents* all right; but not
Christmas.   You know they are Jews."

" Jews ? " said Matilda. " What then ?
What has their being Jews to do with it ? "

" Why ! " said Norton, " don't you know ?
Do you think Jews love Christmas ? You
forget what Christmas is, don't you ? "

" O — I remember.   They don't believe in
Christ," said Matilda in an awed and sorrow-
ful tone.

" Of course.   And that's a mild way to
put it," rejoined Norton. " But grandmamma
will always keep Christmas with all her
might, and aunt Judy too; just because
Davie and Judy don't like it, I believe. So
we have times."

" But how comes it they don't like what
you all like, and their mother ? " Matilda
asked.

" They have Jew relations, you see," said
Norton; " and that goes very much against

the grain with aunt Judy. There is some old Rabbi here in New York that is David's great uncle and makes much of him; and so David has been taught about Jewish things, and told, I suppose, that he must never forget he is a Jew; and he don't, I guess. Not often."

" Is he good ? " asked Matilda.

" Good ? David Bartholomew ? Not particularly. Yes, he is good in a way. He knows how to behave himself."

" Then how is he not good ? "

" He has a mind of his own," said Norton; "and if you try him, you will find he has a temper. I have seen him fight — I tell you! — like that Bengal tiger if *he* was a Jew; when a fellow tried him a little too hard. His mother don't know, and you mustn't tell mamma. The boys let him alone now."

" At school, was it ? " said Matilda.

" At school. You see, fellows try a boy at school, all round, till they find where they can have him; and then he has got to shew what he is made of."

"Do they try you?"

"Well, no; they like me pretty well at St. Giles'."

"And they don't like David?"

"They let him alone," said Norton. "No, they don't like him much. He keeps himself to himself too much for their liking. They would forget he is a Jew, if *he* would forget it; but he never does."

Matilda's thoughts had got into a new channel and ran along fast, till Norton brought them back.

"So we have got to look out for Christmas, Pink, as I told you. It's only just three weeks from to-morrow."

"What then, Norton? What do you do?"

"Everything we can think of," said Norton; "and to begin, everybody in the house gives something to every other body. That makes confusion, I should think!"

"Do *you* give things to your mother? and to Mrs. Lloyd?"

" To every one of 'em," said Norton ; " and it's a job. I shall begin next week to get ready ; and so must you."

Matilda had it on her tongue to say that she had no money and therefore nothing to get ready ; but she remembered in time that if she said that or anything like it, Norton would report and ask for a supply for her. So she held her tongue. But how delightful it must be to get presents for everybody! Not for Mrs. Lloyd, exactly ; Matilda had no special longings to bestow any tokens upon her ; or Mrs. Bartholomew ; but Maria, and Anne, and Letitia! And Norton himself. How she would like to give him something! And if she could, what in the world would it be ? On this question Matilda's fancy fairly went off and lost itself, and Norton got no more talk from her till they reached home.

She mused about it again when she was alone in the carriage that afternoon driving to Mme. Fournisson's. As she had not the money, she thought she might as well have

the comfort of fancying she had it and thinking what she would do with it; and so she
puzzled in delightful mazes of dreamland,
thinking what she would get for Norton if
she had the power. It was so difficult a
point to decide that the speculation gave her
a great deal to do. Norton was pretty well
supplied with things a boy might wish for;
he did not want any of the class of presents
Matilda had carried to Maria. But Norton
was very fond of pretty things. Matilda
knew that; yet her experience of delicate
matters of art was too limited, and her
knowledge of the resources of New York
stores too unformed, to give her fancy much
scope. She had a vague idea that there
were pretty things that he might like, if only
she knew where they were to be found. In
the mean time, it was but the other day, she
had heard him complaining that the guard of
his watch was broken. Matilda knew how
to make a very pretty, strong sort of watch
guard; if she only had some strong brown

silk to weave it of. That was easy to get, and would not cost much; if she had but a few shillings. Those round toed boots! It darted into her mind, how the two dollars and a half she had paid for those round toes, would have bought the silk for a watch guard and left a great deal to spare. There was a little sharp regret just here. It would have been such pleasure! And she would not have been quite empty handed in the great Christmas festival. But the round toes? Could she have done without them?

The question was not settled when she got to the dressmaker's; and for a good while there Matilda could think of nothing but her new dresses and the fashion and style which belonged to them. All that while the dressmaker, not Mme. Fournissons by any means, but one of her women, was trying on the bodies of these dresses, measuring lengths, fitting trimmings, and trying effects. It was done at last; and then Matilda desired the coachman to take her to 316 Bolivar street.

It was very grand, to ride in a carriage all alone by herself; to sink back on those luxurious cushions and look out at the people who were getting along in the world less easily; trudging over the stones and going through the dirt. And it was very pleasant to feel that she had a stock of rich and elegant dresses getting ready for her wear, and such a home of comfort, instead of the old last summer's life at Mrs. Candy's. Matilda was grown strong and well, her cheeks filled out and fresh-coloured; she felt like another Matilda. But as she drove along with these thoughts, the other thought came up to her, of her new opportunities. The Lord's child, — yes, that was not changed; she was that still; what was the work she ought to do, here and now? Opportunities for what, had she? Matilda thought carefully about it. And one thing which she had expected she could do, she feared was going out of her reach. How was she ever to have more money to spare for people needing it, if the demands of her new position kept pace with her increased means? If her boots must always cost seven dollars instead of three, having twice as much money to buy them with would not much help the matter. " And they must," said Matilda to herself. " With such dresses as these I am to have, and in such a house as Mrs. Lloyd's, those common boots I used to wear at Shadywalk would not do at all. And to wear with my red and green silks, I know I must have a new pair of slippers, with bows, like Judy's. I wonder how much *they* will cost? And then I shall hardly have even pennies for the little girls that sweep the street, at that rate."

Opportunities? were all her opportunities gone from her at once? That could not be; and yet Matilda did not see her way out of the question.

So the carriage rolled along with her, and she by and by got tired of thinking and began to examine more carefully into what there was to see. She was coming into a quarter of the city unlike those where she had been before. The house of Mme. Fournissons was in a very quiet street certainly; but what she was passing now was far below that in pretension. *These* streets were very uncomfortable, she thought, even to ride through. Yet the houses themselves were as good and as large as many houses in Shadywalk. But nothing in Shadywalk, no, not Lilac lane itself, was so repelling. Nothing in Shadywalk was so dingy and dark. Lilac lane was dirty, and poor; yet it was broad enough and the cottages stood far enough apart to let the sky look in. Here, in these streets, houses and people seemed to be packed. There was a bare look of want; a forlorn abandonment of every sort of pleasantness; what must it be to go in at one of those doors? Matilda thought; and to live there? — the idea was too disagreeable to dwell upon. Yet people lived there. What sort? Dingy people, as far as Matilda

could see; dirty people, and as hopeless looking as the houses. It was not however a
region of the wretchedly poor through which
her course lay; the windows were whole and
the roofs were decent; but it made the little
girl's heart sick to look at it all, and read the
signs she could not read. Through street
after street of this general character the carriage went; narrow streets, very full of mud
and dirt; where the horses stepped round an
overturned basket of garbage in one place,
and in another stopped for a dray to get out
of their path; where children looked as if
their heads were never brushed, and often
the women looked as if their clothes were
never clean. Matilda could never *walk* to
see her sisters, that was plain; she was glad
nobody was in the carriage with her; and
she was much disappointed to see even a
part of New York look like this.

In a street a little wider, a little cleaner, a
shade or two more respectable, the carriage
stopped at last. It stopped, and Matilda got

16

out. Was this Bolivar street? But she looked and saw that 316 was the number of the house. So she rang the bell.

It was the right place; and she was shewn into a parlour, where she had to wait a little. It was respectable, and yet it oppressed all Matilda's senses. The room was full of buckwheat cake smoke, to begin with, which had filled it that morning and probably every morning of the week, and was never encouraged, nor indeed had ever a chance, to pass away. So each morning made its addition to the stock, till now Matilda felt as if it could be almost seen as well as felt. It certainly was in the carpet, the dingy old brown carpet, in which the worn holes were too many and too evident to be hidden by rug or crumb cloth or concealed by disposition of furniture. It wreathed the lamps on the mantelpiece and the picture on the wall, which last represented a very white monument with a very green willow tree drooping limp tresses over it, and a lady in black press-

ing a white handkerchief to her eyes. An
old mahogany chest of drawers and a table
with some books on it did not help the effect;
for the chest of drawers was out of place,
the cotton table cover was dingy and hung
awry, and the books were soiled and dog's
eared. Matilda felt all this in three minutes; then she forgot it in the joy of seeing
her sisters. The greeting on her part was
very warm; too warm for her to find out
that on their part it was a little constrained.
They were interested enough, however, in all
that had befallen Matilda, to give talk full
flow; and made her tell them the whole story
of the past months; the ship fever, the visit
at Briery Bank, the adoption of herself to be
a child of the house, the coming to New
York, and the composition of the family circle in Mrs. Lloyd's house. The elder sisters
said very little all the while, except to ask
questions.

" And it's for good and all!" said Letitia,
when Matilda had done.

" Yes.   For good and all ! "

" And what is Maria doing ? " said Anne.

" Maria is in Poughkeepsie, you know, learning mantua-making."

" Is she happy ? does she get along well ? "

" I don't know," replied Matilda dubiously. She had not known Maria to seem happy for a very long period ; certainly not at the time of her last visit to her.

" And *we* are here," said Letitia.   " I don't know why all the good should come to Matilda, for my part."

Matilda could say nothing.   It was a dash of cold water.

" I suppose you have everything in the world you want ? " Letitia went on.

" Does she treat you really exactly as if you were her child ? " said Anne.   " Mrs. Laval, I mean."

" Just as if I were," said Matilda.

" And you can have everything you want ? " asked Letitia ; but not as if she were glad of it.

" If Mrs. Laval knows it," said Matilda.

" You can let her know it, I suppose. It ain't fair!" cried Letitia; "it ain't fair! Why should Matilda have all the good that comes to anybody? Here this child can have everything she wants; and you and I, and Maria, have to work and work and pinch and pinch, and can't get it then."

" Is that your dress for every day?" said Anne, after she had lifted Matilda's cloak to see what was underneath.

" I don't know, Anne."

" You don't know? Don't you know what you wear every day?"

" Yes, but I don't know what will be my every day frock. I do not wear the same in the morning and in the afternoon."

" You don't!" said Anne. " How many dresses have you?"

" And what are they?" added Letitia.

Matilda was obliged to tell.

" Think of it!" said Letty. " This child! *She* has silks and cashmeres and reps, more

than she can use; and I, old as I am, haven't
a dress to go to church in, but one that I
have worn a whole winter. I could get one
for twenty shillings, and I haven't money to
spare for that!"

"Hush," said Anne; "we shall do better
by and by, when we have gone further into
the business."

"We shall be delving in the business
though, for it, all the while. And Matilda is
to do nothing and live grand. She'll be too
grand to look at us and Maria."

"Where do you live?" Anne asked.

"It's the corner of 40th street and Blessington Avenue."

Anne's face darkened.

"Where is Blessington Avenue?" asked
Letitia.

"It's away over the other side of the city,"
Anne answered.

"Well, I suppose there is all New York
between us," said Letitia. "Don't you think
this is a delightful part of the town, Matilda?"

"I should think you would go back to Shadywalk, Anne and Letty, when you have learned what you want to learn; it would be pleasanter to make dresses for the people there, wouldn't it, than for people here?"

"Speak for yourself," said Letty. "Do you think nobody wants to be in New York but you?"

"I don't want to live where Mrs. Candy lives," said Anne. "That's enough for me."

"The conversation had got into a very disagreeable channel, where Matilda could not deal with it. Perhaps that helped her to remember that it was getting late and she must go.

"How did you get here?" asked Letitia. "You could not find your way alone. I declare! you don't mean to say that carriage is for you?"

"I couldn't come any other way," said Matilda, as meekly as if it had been a sin to ride in a carriage.

"I declare!" said Letitia. "Look, Anne,

what a carriage. It is a close carriage, just
as handsome as it can be."

" Was nobody with you?" said Anne.

" No, she has it all to herself," said Letitia.
" Well, I hope she'll enjoy it. And I would
be glad of twenty shillings to get a dress to
walk to church in."

Matilda was glad to bid good bye and to
find the carriage door shut upon her. She
was very glad to be alone again. Was it
any wrong in her, that she had so much more
than her sisters? It was not her own doing;
she did not make Mrs. Laval's wealth, nor
gain Mrs. Laval's affection, by any intent
of her own; and further, Matilda could not
understand how Anne and Letitia were any
worse off for her better circumstances. If she
could have helped it, indeed, that would have
been another affair; and here one thorn
pricked into Matilda's heart. She might not
have thought of it if the amount named had
not been just what it was; but twenty shillings? — that was exactly the two dollars

and a half she had paid to be in the fashion as to her toes. Now was it right, or not? Ought she to have those two and a half dollars in hand to give to Letty for her dress? The thorn pricked rather sharp.

CHAPTER VIII.

IT was growing dusk when Matilda got home. She tapped at Mrs. Laval's door before seeking her own.

Mrs. Laval was sitting on a low chair in front of the fire. She had bid " come in," at the knock, and now received Matilda into her arms; and making her sit down on her lap, began taking off her things between kisses.

" You have got home safe and warm," she said, as she pulled off Matilda's glove and felt of the little fingers.

" O yes! I had a beautiful ride," Matilda answered.

" And a pleasant visit ? "

Now the answer to this was not so easy to give. Matilda struggled for an answer, but truth would not find one. Mortification did. She flung her arms round Mrs. Laval's neck and hid her face, for she felt the tears were coming.

"My darling!" said the lady, very much surprised, — "what is the matter? Was it not pleasant?"

But Matilda would not say that either. She let her action speak for her. Mrs. Laval kissed and caressed her, and then when the child lifted up her head, asked in a more business-like tone, "What was it, Matilda?"

"I don't know," — was all that Matilda could say.

"Were they not glad to see you?"

"I thought they were, at first," said Matilda. "I was very glad to see them. Afterwards" —

"Yes, what afterwards?"

"Something was the matter. I think — maybe —they felt a little bad because I have so much more than they have; and I don't deserve it any more."

" I understand," said Mrs. Laval. " I dare say. Well, dear, we will try and find some way of making them feel better. Don't you be troubled. What have you been about all day? I have scarcely seen you. Did you go to Laddler's this morning? "

" Yes, ma'am. Norton took me there."

" And you got your boots, such as you wanted? "

" I got them — I believe so. They are narrow toes."

" Was that what you wanted? " said Mrs. Laval smiling.

" I could have got broad toed boots for a good deal less, but he said they were out of fashion; they were last year's style."

" Yes, he knows," said Mrs. Laval. " Of course he knows, for he makes them."

" Don't other people know? "

" I suppose so," said Mrs. Laval; " but really I never think about it. I take what he gives me and am sure it is all right. That is the comfort of going to Laddler."

" But wouldn't you have found it out, if I had got the square toes ? "

" I might have found it out," said Mrs. Laval laughing, " but I should not have known it was wrong. I should have taken it for the last style."

" Then what difference does it make ? " said Matilda.

" It makes a good deal of difference to the shoemaker," said Mrs. Laval ; " for as often as he can bring in a new fashion he can make people buy new shoes. But how was it at Madame Fournissons ? "

" It was all right," said Matilda. " She tried everything on, and made them all fit."

Mrs. Laval wrapped arms a little closer about the tiny figure on her lap.

" Now do you know," she said, " there is another piece of work you have got to attend to. Has Norton told you about Christmas ? "

" Yes, ma'am ; something."

" You know there is a great time of present

giving. You must take your turn, with the rest. How will you manage it?"

"Manage what, ma'am?"

"Manage to get gifts for all these people? Shall I do it for you?"

"Why I cannot do it," said Matilda simply; "because I have nothing to get them with."

Mrs. Laval laughed and kissed her. "Suppose I supply that deficiency? You could not very well do it without money, unless you were a witch. But if I give you the money, darling? Here are twenty dollars; now you may spend them, or I will spend them for you. Would you like to do it?"

"I would like to do it very much!" said Matilda flushing with excitement, — "if I can."

"Very well. Norton will shew you where pretty things are to be bought, of various sorts. You can get everything in New York. I expect I shall not see you now for three weeks to come; you will be shopping all the time. You have a great deal to do."

Matilda flushed more and more, clasped the notes in her hand, and looked delighted.

" Well, I suppose I must let you go," said Mrs. Laval, " for I must get ready for dinner, and you must. But first, — Matilda, when are you going to call me mamma? This is not to make you forget the mother you had, maybe a better one than I am ; but I am your mother now. I want you to call me so."

Matilda threw her arms round Mrs. Laval's neck again. " Yes — I will," she whispered. There were new kisses interchanged between them, full of much meaning; and then Matilda went up to her room.

At the top of the stairs, in each story, there was a large open space, a sort of lobby, carpeted and warm and bright, into which the rooms opened. Matilda paused when she got to her own, and stood by the rails thinking. The twenty dollars had not at all taken away her regret on the subject of Letitia's dress ; rather the abundance which came pouring in upon her pricked her conscience the more with the contrast between her own case and that of her sister, which a little self-denial on her part would have rendered less painful. Mrs. Laval had unwittingly helped the feeling too by her slight treatment of the matter of the boots; it appeared that she would never have known or cared, if Matilda had got the objectionable square toes. Judy would; but then, was Judy's laugh to be set against Letitia's joy in a new dress? a thing really needed? Matilda could not feel satisfied with her action. When she bought those boots, she had not done it according to her motto; that was the conclusion.

She came to that conclusion before she opened the door of her room; but then she took up the consideration of how the mischief might be remedied; and all the while she was dressing and putting away her walking things, her head in a delightful bustle of thoughts tried different ways of disposing of her money. She must consult Norton; that was the end of it.

" Well," said Norton, when she had a chance to do this after dinner, — " I see what is before us; we have got to go into all the stores in New York between this and Christmas; so we had best begin to-morrow. To-morrow we will go — Do you know what *sort* of things you want, Pink ? "

" Only one or two."

" See now. You must have something for everybody. That is, counting great and small, six persons in this house. Any beside ? "

" O yes; but I know what to do for *them,* Norton; at least I shall know; it is only these that trouble me."

" What will you offer to grandmamma ? "

" I just don't know, Norton ! I can't even imagine."

Norton pondered.

" Hollo, Davy ! " he cried presently. " You and Judy come over here. I want to talk to you."

Judith and her brother came over the room

17

to where Norton and Matilda were. Judith sat down, but David stood waiting.

"The thing is, friends and relatives," Norton began, "how and by what measures we can jointly and severally succeed in distinguishing ourselves, in the matter of our Christmas offerings to Mrs. Lloyd. I want your opinion about it. It is always nearly as much bother as Christmas is worth. The old lady don't want anything, that I ever discovered, and if she did, no one of us is rich enough to relieve her. Now a bright plan has occurred to me. Suppose we club."

"Club what?" said David.

"Forces. That is, put our stock together and give her something clever — from the whole of us, you know."

David looked at the new member of the quartette, as if to see whether she would do to work with; Judy whistled softly.

"What shall we give her?" said that young lady. "She has got everything under the sun already."

" Easier to find one thing than four things, then," said Norton.

" I think it will do," said David. " It is a good idea. And I saw the article at Candello's yesterday."

" What was it ? "

" A liqueur stand. Grandmamma was admiring it. It is very elegant; the shapes of the flasks and cups are so uncommon, and so pretty."

" David is a judge of that," said Norton by way of comment to Matilda. " I go in for colour, and he for shapes."

" There is no colour here," said David; " it is all clear glass."

" The cordial will give the colour," said Norton. " Yes, I think that will do. Hurra! Grandmamma is always on my mind about this time, and it keeps down my spirits."

" Who'll go and get it ? " said Judy.

" We'll all go together," said Norton. " We are *all* going to get it; didn't you understand ? I want to see for myself, for my part, before

the thing's done. I say! let us each give a
glass, and have our names engraved on
them."

"I don't want anybody to drink out of
'Judy,'" said the young lady tossing her head.

"Grandmamma will think she is kissing
you," said Norton. "She'll wear out that
glass, that's the worst of it."

"Then somebody else will have to drink
out of 'David,'" said Judy's brother. "I
don't know about that."

"Well, she'd like it," said Norton.

"But I wouldn't," said Judy. "I have no
objection to her kissing me; but fancy other
people!"

"It won't hurt," said Norton. "You'll
never feel it through the glass. But anyhow,
we'll all go to Candello's to-morrow and see
the thing, and see what we'll do. Maybe
she'll give us cordial in our own cups. That
would be jolly! — if it was noyau."

"You are getting jolly already," said Judith.
"Does Matilda ever get jolly?"

" You'll find out," said Norton; " in course
of time, if you keep your eyes open. But I
don't believe you know a brick when you see
it, Judy."

" A brick ! " said that young lady.

" Yes. There are a great many sorts,
David can tell you. Bricks are a very old
institution. I was studying about Chaldæan
bricks lately. They were a foot square and
two or three inches thick ; and if they were
not well baked they would not stand much,
you know."

" What nonsense you are talking!" said
Judith scornfully.

" Some of those bricks were not nonsense,
for they have lasted four thousand years.
That's what I call — a brick !"

" You wouldn't know it if you saw it
though," David remarked.

" You shut up!" said Norton. " Some of
your ancestors made them for Nebuchadnezzar."

" Some of my ancestors were over the

whole province of Babylon," said David. "But *that* was not four thousand years ago."

"When I get back as far as Nebuchadnezzar," said Norton shutting his eyes, as if in the effort at abstraction, "I have got as far as I can go. The stars of history beyond that seem to me all at one distance."

"They do not seem so to me," said David. "It was long before Nebuchadnezzar that Solomon reigned; and the Jews were an old people then."

"I know!" said Norton. "Nothing can match you but the Celestials. After all, Noah's three sons all came out of the ark together."

"But the nations of Ham are all gone," said David; "and the nations of Japhet are all changing."

"This fellow's dreadful on history?" said Norton to Matilda. "I used to *think*," he went on as the coloured waiter just then came in with coffee, "I used to *think* there were some of Ham's children left yet."

" But not a nation," said David.

The one of Ham's children in question came round to them at this minute, and the talk was interrupted by the business of cream and sugar. The four children were all round the coffee tray, when Mrs. Laval's voice was heard calling Matilda. Matilda went across the room to her.

" Are they giving you coffee, my darling ? " said Mrs. Laval, putting her arm round her.

" I was just going to have some."

" I don't want you to take it. Will it seem very hard to deny yourself ? "

" Why no," said Matilda ; then with an effort, — " No, mamma ; not if you wish me to let it alone."

" I do. I don't want this delicate colour on your cheek," and she touched it as she spoke, " to grow thick and muddy ; I want the skin to be as fair and clear as it is now."

" Norton takes coffee," said Mrs. Bartholomew.

"I know. Norton is a boy. It don't matter."

" Judy!" Mrs. Bartholomew called across
the room, "Judy! don't *you* touch coffee."

" It's so hot mamma, I don't touch it. I
swallow it without touching. It goes right
down."

" I don't like you to drink it."

" It would be a great deal pleasanter to
drink it, than to swallow it in that way," said
Judy, coming across the room with a hop,
skip and jump indescribable. " But coffee
is coffee anyhow. Mayn't I take it a little
cooler and a little slower next time ? "

" It will make your complexion thick."

" It will make my eyes bright, though,"
said Judy unblushingly.

" I never heard that," said Mrs. Bartholomew laughing.

" O but I have, though," said Judy. " I

have seen your eyes ever so bright, mamma,
when you have been drinking coffee."

" Yours are bright enough without it,"
said her mother.

" Yes'm," said Judy contentedly, standing
her ground.

Matilda wondered a good deal at both
mother and daughter, and she was amused
too ; Judy was so funnily impudent, and Mrs.
Bartholomew so lazily authoritative. She
nestled within Mrs. Laval's arm which encir-
cled her, and felt safe, in the midst of very
strange social elements. Mrs. Lloyd eyed
her.

" How old is that child, Zara ? "

" About Judith's age."

" No, she isn't, aunt Zara," said Judy.
" She is about seven years and three
months."

" And what are you ? " said her aunt.

" Judith is over twelve," said Mrs. Bartholomew. " Surely that child is not so
old ? "

" Matilda is the shortest," said Mrs. Laval, looking from one to the other.

" And much the youngest looking," said Mrs. Lloyd. " How do you like New York, my dear ? "

" She likes it," said Judy, — " if she only could have got a black satin cloak."

Matilda stared at her in mingled amazement and shame. Mrs. Laval laughed and hugged Matilda up a little closer.

" A black satin cloak ? " she repeated. " Did you wish for a black satin cloak, my dear ? "

" Trimmed with a deep fall of lace," added Judy.

" O Judy," exclaimed Matilda, " you said nothing about lace ! "   .

" You wanted it, though," said Judith.

" I never thought of such a thing, mamma, as lace," said Matilda appealingly.

" But you did wish for the satin ? "

" Judy seemed to think it would be pretty. She wanted me to ask you to get it."

The shout of laughter which was raised upon this, Matilda did not at all understand. They all laughed, Judy not the least of them. Matilda was very much ashamed.

" Oh Judy, Judy ! " her aunt said. " Matilda, black satin is what old ladies wear. She has been fooling you, as she fools everybody., You mustn't believe Judy Bartholomew in anything she tells you. You would be a little old woman, in a black satin cloak with deep lace."

" She said nothing about lace," Matilda repeated. " But I shall learn what is proper, in her company."

And Matilda's little head, despite her confusion, took the airy set upon her shoulders which was with her the unconscious expression of disdain or disapprobation. There was another burst of laughter.

" Your shoulders are older than your face, my dear," observed Mrs. Lloyd. " Judith must take care what she does. I see there is something in you."

Happily this speech was Greek to Matilda; she had not the least knowledge of what called it forth. However, she took it as a sign that Mrs. Lloyd was beginning to like her a little. All the more she was sorry, as her feet went up the stairs that night, that the way was not clear about the Christmas gift for the stately old lady.

She had meant to speak of it to the other children, but had no chance. After Mrs. Laval called her to tell her about the coffee, the quartette party was broken up; the two boys had left the room and not come back again. So what would have been better disposed of at once, was of necessity laid over to the next day. Matilda had scruples about taking part in a gift that had anything to do with the promotion of drinking. She knew well enough what liqueur was; she had tasted it on the occasion of that first memorable visit she and Maria had made to Mrs. Laval's house; she knew it was very strong, stronger than wine, she thought; for people only drank it out of little glasses that would not hold much more than a good thimbleful. She had seen it once or twice already at Mrs. Lloyd's served after dinner. She had seen David and Norton and Judy all take it. Now she herself was pledged to do all she could in the cause of temperance. Her all would not be much here, something said to her; nobody would mind what she thought or said; true. Nevertheless, ought she not to do *what she could?* according to her old motto. And following her new motto, to " do all in the name of the Lord Jesus," could she rightly join, even silently, in a plan to make a present of drinking flasks and glasses? But if she refused, what a fuss it would make!

Matilda went slowly up the stairs thinking of it; and arrived in her room, she turned on the gas and opened her Bible and sat down to study the question. She found she could not read, any more than those few strong words; they seemed to cover the whole

ground ; " Whatsoever ye do, in word or
deed, do all in the name of the Lord Jesus."
Could she, as his little servant, help the other
children in giving such a gift? And she
was pledged, as a member of the Commission
no less than as a servant of Christ, to do all
she could for the cause of temperance.
Would it not be *something* for the cause of
temperance, if she declared off from having
anything to do with the liqueur stand ? She
had felt she must try somehow to speak to
David and Norton about their own drinking
wine ; this was a good chance, and if she let
this chance go — I can never do it another
time, she thought to herself. But oh, the
difficulty and the pain of it ! They thought
her a baby, and a little country girl, who
knew nothing ; they would laugh at her so,
and perhaps be angry too. How could she
do it ! And once or twice Matilda put her
head down on her book in the struggle, wish-
ing with all her heart it were not so hard to
be a Christian.

But all her thoughts and her prayers only made her more and more sure which way lay the course of duty; and along with that grew a heavy looking forward to the next day and the trial it would bring. How to manage the matter best was a question. To speak privately to Norton alone would be far the easiest; but then, that might not secure the effect of her protest against wine and cordials and all such things, as she wished to make it; Norton would perhaps cover it up, for the sake of shielding her and himself from the reproaches of the others; and so the work would not be done. She could not decide. She was obliged to go to bed and leave it to circumstances to open the way for her. She half made up her mind that the "opportunities" of her new position were as likely to be opportunities for self denial as for anything else. This was not what she had expected.

Saturday morning rose still and fair. The wind had gone down; the severe cold had abated; the weather was beautifully prosperous for the children's expedition. Now if Matilda could get a chance to speak before they set out — It would be awkward to have to speak in the store, maybe before a shopman, and when they were all on the very point of finishing what they came to do. Matilda was ready to wish the day had been stormy; and yet she wanted to go to Tiffany's, where Norton had said he would take her; and to Candello's too, for the matter of that.

There was another question Matilda had to settle with herself, only she could not attend to so many things at once. Her twenty dollars for Christmas purchases; how was all *that* to be spent "in the name of the Lord Jesus"? She could not think of it just now, except by snatches; she kept remembering it, and trying to reckon how many people she had to buy things for. New York certainly was a very puzzling place to live in.

The other children seemed to be as full of

business as she, and much less quiet about it. So Matilda did not find a chance to speak to Norton in private, which in her trouble she would have done if she could. It was all bustle and discussion till they went to get ready for their walk. Matilda laced on her new boots. Judy won't have any occasion to look scornfully at those, she said to herself. They are as nice as they can be.

A little to her surprise, when she got down-stairs she found Miss Judy dressed in a black silk pelisse. What was the difference be-tween silk and satin, Matilda wondered? Judy caught her glance perhaps, for with a twinkle of her own sharp black eyes she burst out into a peal of laughter.

"What is the matter now?" her brother asked.

"Things become people so differently," said Judith saucily. "Something you couldn't understand, Davy; men don't; nor boys neither. Matilda and I understand."

"Matilda don't understand much that you do," said Norton.

" An' that's thrue for ye!" said Judy with
a strong Irish accent. " Faith, the craythur,
she's just innicent!"

" Hush, Judy," said her brother laughing;
and " You're a case, Judy," said Norton; and
so they went out at the front door. Matilda's
opportunity was gone; she had thought to
speak out to them all while they were in the
hall; and now she was a little too vexed to
speak, for a while. However, it was a gay
walk down the avenue and then down Broadway. The day was very fine and all the
world seemed to be out and astir. Norton
was talking very busily too, and the excitement of business soon chased away the mo-
mentary excitement of displeasure. In the
midst of all this, every few blocks they came
to street sweepers. A little girl or a little
boy, grey and ragged, keeping a clean crossing and holding out eager little hands for the
pennies they did not get. David and Norton
and Judith did not so much as look at the children, passing the outstretched hands as if un-

seen ; and Matilda had no pennies ; nothing
but her twenty dollar bill. Every few blocks
there was one of these poor, grey dusty figures and one of those little empty hands.
Matilda might have forgotten one or two,
if that had been all ; it was impossible to forget this company. How came their life to be
so different from her life ? What a hard way
to spend one's days! always at a street corner. And where did they hide themselves at
night ? And did any of those poor little ones
ever know what Christmas meant ? And
most of all, what could or ought she to do for
them, she who had so much ? What could
be squeezed out of those twenty dollars to
refresh the corners of the streets ? anything ?

Thinking about this, and replying to Norton, and finding her way among the crowds
of people, they had come to Candello's before
Matilda had found a time to speak anything
of what was chiefly on her mind.

It was a long bright store, elegant with its
profusion of beautiful things in glass and por-

celain and bronze. Every foot of the counters and of the floor, along the sides of the
room, seemed to Matilda to be filled with
things to be looked at. Such beautiful ba-
sins and ewers, just for washing! Such
charming vases and flower glasses! Such
handsome clocks and statuettes and lamps!
Then there were painted cups, and flowered
goblets and tumblers, and flasks wonderfully
cut, and bowls, large and beautiful, but
clearly not for toilet use, that excited Matilda's wonderment. She was lost in delight
as well as wonder.

"Here," said David, and the word struck
like a blow upon her nerves of hearing, —
"here is the article. Isn't that unexception-
able now?"

With the others, Matilda turned to see
what he was pointing at. A glass liqueur
stand, with a crystal flask and tiny cups to
match; as pretty and elegant as it could be;
even rare in its delicate richness among so
many delicate and rich things. The others

were eager in their praise. Matilda was silent.

"Don't you like it, Pink?" said Norton.

"It is as pretty as it can possibly be," Matilda answered. "But Norton"—

"Then we might as well get it," said Norton. "We're all agreed. There's no use in looking further when you are suited."

"So I think," said David. "I never do."

"That is as good as Mrs. Lloyd could do for herself," said Judith.

"But Norton"—said Matilda.

"Shall we have our names put on the cups?" said Norton.

"But Norton," said Matilda desperately, "we are *not* all agreed. I am very sorry!— I like it very much — it's beautiful"—

"You are afraid you haven't money enough?" said Norton. "Never fear! Davy and I will pay the largest half; you and Judy shall give less, but it don't make any difference. I'll tell you! David and I will get the stand and the flask; and you two shall give the cups."

"It isn't that," said Matilda, very much distressed; "it is not that, Norton; it is something else. It is" —

"What in the world is it?" said Judy, balancing herself daintily on one toe.

"It is — that I don't drink wine, you know."

"What's that to do?" said Judy, while the two boys both looked at Matilda. "*You* haven't to drink or let it alone; it is not for your use anyhow."

"No, I know that; but I don't think it is right — I mean, — I mean," said Matilda, gathering courage, "I have promised to do all I can to prevent people from drinking wine. I can't help in such a present as this."

"They don't drink wine out of these little cups," said David. "It is something different; it is Noyau, or Curaçoa, or Chartreuse, or Maraschino, or some of those things, you know."

" Yes, but it is stronger," said Matilda in a low voice. " It's stronger than wine."

" She's temperance!" exclaimed Judith, turning round on one heel and coming back into position. " She's temperance! We are all wicked at Mrs. Lloyd's; we drink Hock and we sip Curaçoa. I suppose she has only been where people drink gin and lager; and she thinks it's all alike."

" She has been at Briery Bank, Judy," said Norton, " where the wines are as good as in Blessington Avenue."

" Then she ought to have learned better!" said Judy. " That's all I have to say."

" But Pink," said Norton, and he was very kind, though he looked vexed, — " this is not anything about *your* drinking or not drinking, you know. Grandmamma will have her wine and she will offer her cordial, just the same; it don't make any difference; only we want to give her something she will like, and she will like this; don't you see ?"

" Yes, Norton, I see," said Matilda, her

eyes filling with tears; " I am *very* sorry ; but I wish you and David wouldn't have any- thing to do with wine, either."

" She don't mention *me*!" exclaimed Judy. " Either I'm so good I'm safe; or I'm so bad it's no use trying to take care of me. You poor boys, she will try to take care of *you*. What impertinence!"

" No more than if you did it, Judy, come, now!" said Norton. " It's no such thing; it's only nonsense. Now Pink, *don't* be nonsensical!"

" We can do it without her being in the affair, if she doesn't like it," said David. " But I do not understand," he went on, ad- dressing himself to Matilda. " Giving a present isn't drinking wine, is it?"

" No," said Matilda, who by this time could hardly speak at all. " But Mr. David, it is helping somebody else to drink."

" Do you think what you do would help or hinder?"

" What *you* do might."

" We shall go on just the same, whatever way you take. What difference can it make, whether your money is in it or not ? " .

" I don't know," said Matilda struggling; — " none, perhaps, whether my money is in it. But my *name* would be in it."

" Do you think that would make any difference ? — stop, Norton, I want to understand what she will say. What would your name do, in it or out of it ? "

" Ridiculous ! to spend time talking to her !" said Judy. " That is just what she wants."

But David waited for his answer; and Matilda's eyes were all glittering, while her little head took its inexpressible air of self-assertion.

" I don't know — I can't tell," she said, answering David as if she had not heard Judy; — " it might do nothing, but I have promised to use it on the right side."

" Promised whom ?" said David. " Maybe it is a promise that need not stand. Promised whom ? "

" Yes, whom did you promise, Pink ? "
said Norton.

Matilda hesitated and then spoke.

" I promised the Lord Jesus Christ," she
said slowly.

She was looking at nobody in particular,
yet her eye caught the expression of annoyance on Norton's face; she did not see the
cloud of disgust and surprise that came over
David's. He turned away. Judith's eyes
snapped.

" Isn't that neat now ? " she said. " We
have got a saint among us, sure enough.
Well — saints know how to take care of their
money; we all know that. What are we
poor sinners going to do for grandmamma's
present ? that's the question. I propose that
we get her a prayerbook, very large, and
black, with gilt clasps and her name on the
cover; then everybody will know that Mrs.
Lloyd is a good woman and goes to church."

" Be still, Judy ! " said her brother sternly.

" Propose something yourself then," said

Judith. "We can't do anything at Candello's, that's clear. I don't believe there's
an innocent thing here beside tea cups. I've
seen people drink brandy and water in tumblers; and bowls hold whiskey punch. Dear
me! what a pity it is that good things are so
bad!"

"Hush, Judy!" said Norton; "*you* won't
hurt anybody by being too good."

"It's a way I despise," said Judith coolly.
"When I hurt anybody, I like to know it.
I never shut my eyes and fire."

"It's a wonder you don't take better aim,
then," said Norton impatiently. "You are
firing wild just now. Matilda has a right to
think as she likes, and *she* don't shut her eyes
and fire. There's nothing of a coward about
her. But then we don't think as she thinks,
about some things; and I say we'll get this
liqueur stand and she shall find something
else for her part."

"I'll tell all about it, though, at home,"
said Judy.

" I dare say Matilda would as lieve you did," said Norton. " Come, David — will you finish this business ?   You and I and Judy will go thirds in it.   I've got some other matters to attend to with Matilda, and time is running away; and Monday school begins. Come, Pink — we have got to go to Tiffany's."

" What o'clock is it, Norton ? " Matilda asked as soon as they were outside of the shop.

" Near twelve, Pink.   I declare ! time *does* run."

" Norton, couldn't we go home first, and go to Tiffany's after luncheon ?_ there'll be a long afternoon, you know."

" Every place is so crowded in the afternoon," said Norton. " But you want to go home, Pink ? Well, you shall. We shouldn't have much time before luncheon, that's a fact."

So they got into a street car that was passing.

" Whatever made you say that, Pink ? "
Norton burst out when they were seated.
" David and Judy are set against you
now."

" I think they were before, Norton."

" No, they weren't ; or if they were, I don't
care ; they had nothing to say. Now you
have given them a handle."

" I didn't say anything · very bad," said
Matilda with her voice trembling a little.

" No, but they'll take it so. What is it to
us, what grandmamma, or any one else, does
with a thing after we have given it? *That*
is none of our affair. We only make the
present."

" It would be very strange, though, to give
anybody something you were not willing he
should use," said Matilda.

" Of course. I am willing. I don't care
what anybody does with a thing, after *I* have
done with it."

" I care," said Matilda softly.

" Why ? Now Pink, you don't. What do

you care whether grandmamma drinks curaçoa or not after dinner ? ”

Matilda hesitated.

“ I wish she wouldn't,” she said then
again softly. “ Then you and David and
Judy wouldn't.”

“ Why shouldn't we ? ” said Norton rather
shortly.

“ Because, people get too fond of such
things. And it ruins them.”

“ It hasn't ruined me yet,” said Norton.

But that was about as far as Matilda
could go, and she burst into tears. She kept
them back bravely, while they were in the
car, but she could not find voice to reply to
any of Norton's kind words, which were
meant to be very soothing; and as soon as
they got home she went straight to her room.
Norton went to his mother.

“ We have had a splendid confounded
time ! mamma,” he burst out.

“ Splendid and confounded ? ” his mother
repeated.

" No, ma'am. Splendidly confounded, I
should have said. We went to get grandmamma's present. And Pink, she has contrived to make David and Judy as mad with
her as they can be; and that's saying a good
deal, when you are talking English. Now
how it's to be undone, I don't know. I suppose Pink is crying her eyes out about it.
She had no heart to go to Tiffany's or anything. We are going after dinner, though."

" But what is the matter? what has she
done, Norton? "

" Came out with temperance and *religion*,
and all that sort of thing, to David and Judy;
fancy it, mamma! and more than that, with
the very part of religion that they like least
of all. Wouldn't help us buy a liqueur stand
for grandmamma, because she doesn't think
it is right to use cordials."

" What a child! " exclaimed Mrs. Laval.

" She's got pluck," said Norton, picking up
a pin from the floor and energetically giving
it a cast into the fire; " she's a brick, she is!

I knew that the first day I saw her; but mamma, she is very soft in that spot."

Mrs. Laval looked sober. Perhaps she remembered that the late Mr. Laval had also been soft in that spot, though in an entirely different way. Perhaps she recollected how many variously shaped glasses were needed around his dinner plate, and how he carried about a strong breath and a red face for hours afterward, and how she had been sometimes ever so little ashamed of him. She was now silent.

" Mamma. can't you talk to her ? " Norton began again.

" About what ? " said Mrs. Laval starting.

" This, ma'am ; and make her a little more like other people."

" I would just as lieve she wouldn't drink wine, Norton ; or you either."

" Or grandmamma either, mamma ? "

" You have nothing to do with that. Your grandmamma is an old lady. I am not talking of grandmamma, but of you."

" Well do you want Matilda to preach temperance, ma'am ? "

" You let Matilda alone. She will not go far wrong. She is *never* forward. Was she to-day ? "

" No," said Norton laughing a little; " it was like a small canary bird chirping out a lecture."

" You let her alone," Mrs. Laval repeated; " and don't let the others plague her. And go get yourself ready to go to the table, my boy; the time for luncheon is very near."

" I can't help Judy's plaguing her," said Norton as he turned to go. " David won't do anything. But won't he hate her, from now ! "

CHAPTER IX.

NORTON ran off upstairs. His mother waited till he was safe in his room and then followed him. But she stopped at Matilda's door and softly went in. Matilda's hat was off; that was all; and on her knees beside a chair the little girl was, with bowed head, and sobbing. Mrs. Laval's arms came round her, gently drew her up and enfolded her. "What is all this?" she whispered.

Matilda's face was hid.

"What's the matter, my darling?" Mrs. Laval repeated. "Norton has told me all about it — there is nothing for you to cry about."

"Is he angry with me?" Matilda whispered.

"Angry with you! No, indeed. Norton

could not be that. And there is nothing else you need mind."

" I am very sorry!" said poor Matilda. " I hurt all their pleasure this morning, and they thought I was — very disagreeable, I believe."

" Nobody ever thought that yet," said Mrs. Laval laughing a little; "and no harm is done. It was nonsense for them to get you into that business at all. It is all very well for them to give their grandmother a present; but for you it is quite needless; it is her place to give to you, and not yours to give to her; the cases are different. Norton forgot that."

" Then she will not think it strange that I am not in it?" said Matilda lifting up her face at last.

" Not at all. It would be more strange if you were in it."

" Norton proposed it."

" Yes, I know; but Norton is not infallible. He has made a mistake this time."

" But I offended them, mamma," said Matilda.

"They will get over it. Now dry your
eyes and take your coat off, and we will go
down to luncheon."

They went down together, and Mrs. Laval
took care that no annoyance came to Matilda
during the meal. So after luncheon she was
all ready to take a new start with Norton for
Tiffany's.

"You see, Pink," said Norton as they were
riding down, "all you have to do is to let
people go their own way, and you go your's.
That's all. That's the way so many carts get
through the streets. It isn't necessary to
knock up against every one you come to;
and people don't like it."

"I was only going my own way, Norton,"
Matilda said gently; "but I had to give the
reason for it; and that was what you all
didn't like."

"Your reason interfered with our way,
though," said Norton. "You as good as said
it is wrong to do something we all do."

"Well," said Matilda very slowly,—"ought

you not to try to hinder people from doing
what is not right?"

"How do you know what is not right?"
said Norton.

"The Bible tells."

"Where does the Bible say it is wrong to
drink wine?" Norton asked quickly.

"I'll shew you when we get home."

"Everybody does it, anyhow," said Norton;
"and one must do what everybody does."

"Mr. Richmond don't, Norton."

"Mr. Richmond! He's a minister."

"Well! Other people ought to be as good
as ministers."

"They *can't*," said Norton. "Besides —
Mr. Richmond is all very well; he's a brick;
but then he is not a fashionable man, and he
don't know the world."

"Are ministers ever fashionable men?"
said Matilda, opening her eyes a little.

"Certainly. Why not. Dr. Blandford likes
a good glass of wine as well as any one, and
knows how to drink it. He likes a good
dinner too."

"What do you mean, Norton? Anybody knows how to drink a glass of wine."

"Everybody don't know how to drink half a dozen glasses, though," said Norton. "A wine may be out of place; and it is not good out of place."

"You take it at dinner," said Matilda.

"Yes, but different wines at different times of the dinner," said Norton. "Everything in its place, as much as everything in its own glass, and much more. For instance, you take light wines with the soup; Hock, or Sauterne, or grandmamma's favorite Greek wine. Then champagne with the dinner. Port goes with the cheese. Then claret is good with the fruit; and sherry and madeira with the dessert, or any time. And Dr. Blandford likes a bowl of whiskey punch to finish off with."

"Is he your minister?"

"Dr. Blandford? yes. That is, he's grandmamma's."

"Do you think he is as good as Mr. Richmond?"

" He's better, for a dinner party," said Norton. " He knows what's what, as well as anybody. Now Pink, jump out; here we are."

The stately brown-fronted store struck Matilda with a certain sense of awe. Dr. Blandford was forgotten for the present. She followed Norton in, and stood still to take breath.

" Now," said Norton, " what shall we look at first? What do you want? How many things have you got to get, anyhow, Pink?"

" You know how many people there are at home. Then there are two or three others I have to think of."

" Hm! — seven or eight, I declare," said Norton. " Well, let us walk round and see everything generally."

There were a good many people who seemed to be doing just that; besides a crowd who were undoubtedly purchasers. Slowly Norton and Matilda began their round of the counters. Very slowly they went; for the loads of rich plate were a great marvel to the

unused eyes of the little girl.   She had to beg
a great deal of explanation from Norton as to
the use and meaning of different articles.
Pitchers and tureens and forks and spoons she
could understand; but what could possibly
be the purpose of a vast round vase, with
doves sitting opposite each other on the lip of
it? doves with frosted wings, most beautiful
to behold.

"That?" said Norton. "That's a punch
bowl."

"A punch bowl! And how much would
that cost, Norton?"

"Do you want it?   Too much for your
purse, Pink.   That is marked two hundred
and fifty dollars."

"For a punch bowl!" said Matilda.

"Yes, why not?"

But Matilda did not say why not.   What
must be the rest of the dinner, when the punch
bowl was two hundred and fifty dollars?

"And here's an épergne," said Norton.
"That is to stand in the centre of the dinner

table — for ornament. That's seven hundred and fifty."

" What's inside of the punch bowl, Norton ? it is yellow."

" Gold," said Norton. " It is lined with gold — gold washed, that is. Gold don't tarnish, you know."

They went on. It was a progress of wonders, to Matilda. She was delighted with some wood carvings. Then highly amused with a show of seals ; Norton wished to buy one, and it took him some time to be suited. Then Norton made her notice a great variety of useful articles in morocco and leather and wood; satchels and portemonnaies, and dressing boxes, and portfolios and card cases ; and chains and rings and watches. Bronzes and jewellery held them finally a very long time. The crowd was great in the store ; people were passing in and passing out constantly ; the little boys the door-openers were busy opening and shutting all the time. At last they let out Matilda and Norton.

" Now, Pink," said the latter, well pleased,
" do you know what you want? Have you
seen anything you want? "

" O yes, Norton; a great many things; but
it is all confusion in my head till I think
about it at home."

" We have got other places to go to," said
Norton. " Don't decide anything till you
have seen more. We can't go anywhere else
to-day though. We've got to go home to
dinner."

Matilda's head was in a whirl of pleasure.
For amidst so many beautiful things she was
sure she could do Christmas work charmingly; and at any rate it was delightful only
to look at them. She tried to get her
thoughts a little in order. For Norton, she
would make the watch guard; that was one
thing fixed. A delicate bronze paperweight,
a beautiful obelisk, had greatly taken her
fancy, and Norton had been describing to her
the use of its originals in old Egypt; it was
not very costly, and Matilda thought she

would like to give that to Mrs. Laval. But she would not decide till she saw more; and for her sisters, and for everybody else indeed, she was quite uncertain yet what to choose. She thought about it so hard all the evening that she was able to throw off the gloom of David and Judy's darkened looks.

Next day, however, she had too much time to think. It was Sunday. Matilda was up in good time, as usual, and came down for breakfast; but there was no breakfast and nobody to eat it, till the clock shewed the half hour before ten. Bells had been ringing long ago for Sunday school, and had long ago stopped. Matilda was so hungry, that breakfast when it came made some amends for other losses; but then it was church time. And to her dismay she found that nobody was going to church. The long morning had to be spent as it could, with reading and thinking. Matilda persuaded Norton to take her to church in the afternoon, that she might know the way.

"It don't pay, Pink," said Norton; "however, I'll go with you, and you can see for yourself."

Matilda went and saw. A rich, splendid, luxuriously furnished church; a warm close atmosphere which almost put her to sleep; and a smooth-tongued speaker in the pulpit, every one of whose easy going sentences seemed to pull her eyelids down. Matilda struggled, sat upright, pinched her fingers, looked at the gay colours and intricate patterns of a painted window near her, and after all had as much as she could do to keep from nodding. She was very glad to feel the fresh air outside again.

"Well," said Norton. "Do you feel better?"

"Is that Dr. Blandford?"

"That is he. A jolly parson, ain't he?"

"The church was so warm," said Matilda.

"*He* keeps cool," said Norton. "That's one thing about Dr. Blandford. "You always know where to have him."

"I wish Mr. Richmond was here," said Matilda.

The wish must have been strong; for that very evening, when she went to her room, earlier than usual because everybody was ready to go to bed Sunday night, she wrote a letter to her minister at Shadywalk.

"BLESSINGTON AVENUE, Dec. 6, 18—

"DEAR MR. RICHMOND, — I am here, you see, and I am very happy; but I am very much troubled about some things. Everything is very different from what it was at Shadywalk, and it is very difficult to know what is right to do. So I think I had better ask you. Only there are so many things I want to ask about, that I am afraid my letter will be too long. Sometimes I do not know whether the trouble is in myself or in the things; I think it is extremely difficult to tell. Perhaps you will know; and I will try to explain what I mean as clearly as I can.

" One thing that puzzles me is this. Is it wrong to wish to be fashionable? and how can one tell just how much it is wrong, or right. Mrs. Laval is having some beautiful clothes made for me; ever so many; silks and other dresses; they will be made and trimmed as fashionable people have them; and I cannot help liking to have them so. I am afraid, perhaps, I like it too much. But how can I tell, Mr. Richmond? There is another little girl in the house here, Mrs. Laval's niece; about as old as I am, or not much older; and she has all her things made in these beautiful ways. Is it wrong for me to wish to have mine as handsome as hers? because I do; and one reason why I am so glad of mine is, that I shall be as fashionable as she is. She calls people who are not fashionable, ' country people.'

" There is another thing. Having things made in this way costs a great deal of money. I don't know about that. The other day I paid two dollars more than I need, just to have the toes of my boots right. You would not understand that; but the fashion is to have them narrow and rounded, and last year they were square and wide. And it is so of other things. I buy my own boots and gloves; and I could save a good deal if I would buy the shapes and colours that are not fashionable. What ought I to do? and how can I tell? It troubles me very much.

" I think that is the most of what troubles me, that and spending my money; but that is part of it. I don't want to be unlike other people. Is that wrong, or is it pride? I didn't know but it was pride, partly; and then I thought I would ask you.

" Another thing is, ought I to speak to people about what they do that is not right? I don't mean grown up people, of course; but the boys and Judy. I don't like to do it; but yet I thought I must, as I had promised to do all I could in the cause of temperance; and I did, and some of them were very much offended. They drink wine a great deal here, and I did not like to see Norton do it. So I spoke, and I don't think it did any good.

"My letter is getting very long, but there is one other thing I want to ask about. There are a great many poor children in the streets; boys and girls; *so* dirty that you cannot imagine it; they sweep the street crossings. What can I do for them? Ought I not to give pennies always? all I can?

"I believe that is all. O and I wish you could tell me what to do Sundays. The people here do not care about going to church; and I have been once and I don't wonder. I could hardly keep my eyes open. I miss the Sunday school and you very much. I wish I could see you. Give my love to Miss Redwood. Your affectionate

"MATILDA ENGLEFIELD.

"It will be Matilda Laval after this, but I thought I would sign my own old name once more."

This letter was duly posted the next day. And almost as soon as the mails up and down made it possible, Matilda received her answer.

"SHADYWALK PARSONAGE, Dec. 8, 18—.

" MY DEAR LITTLE TILLY, — I appreciate your difficulties to the full. They *are* difficulties, enough to puzzle an older head than yours. Yet I think there is a simple way out of them, not through your head however so much as your heart. Keep *that* right, and I think we can get at the answer to your questions.

" The answer to them all is, Live by your motto. ' *Whatsoever* ye do, in word or deed, do all in the name of the Lord Jesus.' Try everything by this rule. In spending your money, in deciding between boot-tips and dollars, in the question of reproving wrong in others, in the matter of kindness to the street-sweepers, put your motto before you; and ask yourself, how would the Lord Jesus do if he were here in person and had the same point to decide? The answer to that

20

will tell you how, doing in his name, you ought to act yourself. Pray for direction; and whether you dress or speak or spend money, take care that it is Christ you are trying to please — not yourself, nor yet Miss Judy; but indeed let it be your best pleasure to please Him.

"Now as to your Sundays. If your people do not go to church regularly, you can probably do what you like on Sunday afternoons. Go up your avenue two blocks, turn down then to your right for two blocks more, and you will come to a plain looking brick building, not exactly like a church, nor like a common house. There is Mr. Rush's Sunday school. Go in there, and you will find work and pleasure. And then write again to

"Your very affectionate friend,

"F. RICHMOND."

It would be hazardous to say how many times Matilda read this letter. I am afraid some tears were shed over it. For to tell truth, difficulties rather thickened upon the little girl this week. In the first place, Norton was away at school almost all day. David and he came home to luncheon, which now became the dinner time of the young ones; but even so, he was full of his studies and his mates, and his new skates, and the merits of different styles of those instruments, and Matilda could hardly get anything out of him. David talked little; but he was always more self-absorbed. And with Judy, this week, Matilda had nothing to do. That young lady ignored her. Matilda went out shopping a good deal with Mrs. Laval; that was her best resource. The shops were an unfailing amusement and occupation; for everywhere she had her Christmas work to think of, and everywhere accordingly she kept her eyes open and studied what was before her; weighed the merits and noted the prices even of stuffs and ribbands; and left nothing unexamined that eyes could examine in the fancy stores. And when she got home, Matilda went to her room and made notes of the things she had seen and liked that she thought might be good for a present to one or another of the friends she had to reckon for. The obelisk held its place in her favour for Mrs. Laval; but with respect to the other people a crowd of images filled her imagination. Japanese paperweights, and little tea-pots; so pretty, Matilda thought she *must* buy one; ivory and Scotch plaid and carved wood paper knives, and one with a deer's foot handle. Little Shaker work-baskets, elegantly fitted up; scent-bottles; a carved wood letter-holder at Goupil's; a bronze standish representing a country well with pole and bucket. At Goupil's, where Mrs. Laval had business to attend to, Matilda's happy eyes were full of treasure. She wandered round the room gazing at the pictures, in a dream of delight; finding soon some special favourites which she was sure to revisit with fresh interest every time she had a chance; and Mrs. Laval took her there several times. Once Mrs. Laval, having finished what she came to do, was at a loss where to find Matilda; and only after going half round the long gallery, discovered her, wrapt in contemplation, standing before a large engraving which hung high above her on the wall. Matilda's head was thrown back, gazing; her two little hands were carelessly crossed at her back; she was a sort of picture herself. Mrs. Laval came up softly.

" What are you looking at, my darling ? "

Matilda started. " Have you got through, mamma ? did you want me ? "

" I have got through; but I do not want you unless you are ready. What have you found that pleases you ? "

" Look, mamma. That one — the woman holding a lamp — don't you see ? "

It was Holman Hunt's figure of the woman searching for the lost piece of money.

" What is it ? " said Mrs. Laval.

" Don't you remember, mamma ? the story

of the woman who had ten pieces of silver
and lost one of them? how she swept the
house, and looked until she found it?"

"If I had nine left, I should not take so
much trouble," said Mrs. Laval.

"Ah, but, mamma, you know the Lord
Jesus does not think so."

"The Lord!   *What* are you talking of, my
child?"

"O you do not remember, mamma!   It is
a parable.   The Lord Jesus means us to
know how *he* cares for the lost ones."

Mrs. Laval looked from Matilda to the
picture and back again.

"Do you like it so very much?" she said.

"O I do, mamma! it's beautiful.   What
an odd lamp she has."

"That is the shape lamps used to be," said
Mrs. Laval.   "Not so good as ours."

"Prettier," said Matilda.   "And it seems
to give a good light.   No, it don't, though;
it shines only on a little place.   But it's
pretty."

"You do love pretty things," said Mrs. Laval laughing. "We will come and look at it again."

Matilda, it shewed how enterprising she was getting to be, had already privately inquired the price of the picture. It was fifteen dollars without a frame. Far up over her little head indeed. She drew a long breath, and came away.

The latter part of the week another engrossment appeared, in the shape of her new dresses from Mme. Fournissons. Mrs. Laval tried them all on; and Matilda's head had almost more than it could stand. So many, so handsome, so elegantly made and trimmed, so very becoming they were; it was like a fairy tale. To these dresses Mrs. Laval had been all the week adding riches of under-clothing; a supply so abundant that Matilda had never dreamed of the like, and so elegant and fine in material and make as she had never until then even seen. Now Matilda had a natural liking for extreme neatness and particularity in all that concerned her little person; and to have such plenty of things to wear, so nice of their kind, and full liberty to put them on clean and fresh as often as she pleased, fulfilled her utmost notions of what was desirable. Her mental confusion arose from the articles furnished by Mme. Fournissons. The lustre of the silk, the colour of the blue, the richness of the green, the ruffles, the costly buttons, the tasteful trimmings, the stylish make, all raised a whirl in Matilda's mind. She was a little intoxicated. Nobody saw it; she was very demure about it all; made no show of what she felt; all the same she felt it. She could not help a deep satisfaction at being dressed to the full as well as Judy; a feeling that was not lessened by a certain sense that the satisfaction was on her part alone. Of the two, that is. Mrs. Laval openly expressed hers. Mrs. Lloyd nodded her dignified head and remarked, " That child will do you no discredit, Zara." Mrs. Bartholomew looked at her, which was much;

and Norton declared that from a pink she had bloomed out into a carnation. All these things Matilda felt; and unconsciously in all that concerned dress and equipment she began to set a new standard for herself. One thing must match with another. " Of *course,* I must have round-toed boots," she said to herself now. She began to doubt whether she must not get at least one pair of gloves more elegant than any she found at Shady-walk, to go with her silk dresses and her new coat. She hesitated still, for the price was a dollar and a quarter.

Upon all this came Mr. Richmond's letter; and Matilda found it did not exactly fit her mood of mind. She was confused already, and this made the confusion worse. Then Saturday came; and Norton was free; and he and Matilda made another round of shop-going. The matter was growing imminent now; Christmas would be in a fortnight. But the difficulty of deciding upon the choice of presents seemed as great as ever. Seeing

more things to choose from, only increased
the difficulty. They went this morning to
Stewart's, to find out what might be displayed upon the variety counter; they went
to a place where Swiss carvings were shewn;
finally they went to Anthony's; and they
could not get away from this last place.

" It's long past one o'clock, Pink," said
Norton as they were going down the stairs.

" What shall we do, Norton? I'm very
hungry."

" So am I. One can always do something
in New York. We'll go and have dinner."

" At home ? "

" No indeed. Short of home. We'll jump
into an omnibus and be at the place in a
minute."

It did not seem much more, and they went
into a restaurant and took their places at a
little marble table, and Norton ordered what
they both liked; oyster pie and coffee.

" But mamma does not like me to drink
coffee," said Matilda suddenly.

" No harm, just for once," said Norton. " She would let you, if she was here, I know."

" But she isn't here, and I don't like to do it, Norton."

" I have ordered it. You'll have to take it," said Norton. " Judy takes it every night, and her mother does not wish her to have any." ·

" What then ? " said Matilda.

" Nothing; only that you two are not much alike."

" David don't look at me any more, since last week," said Matilda. " Do you suppose he never will again ? "

" No hurt if he don't," said Norton. " He has *my* leave. Well, Pink, what are you going to get ? "

" I don't know a bit, Norton — except one or two things. I am certain of nothing else but just one or two."

" I am going to get that ring for mamma ; that's fixed. The one with that pale malachite. Grandmamma is disposed of. Then

for aunt Judy a box of French bon-bons. I
think I'll give Davy a standish — I haven't
picked it out yet; but I don't know about
Judy.   It's hard to please her, I never did but
once."

"Then I shall not," said Matilda.

"And it doesn't matter, either.   Here's
your coffee, Pink; and here's mine." .

But after a little struggle with herself, Matilda pushed her cup as far away as she could,
and drew the glass of ice-water up to her
plate instead.   The dinner was good enough,
even so; and Norton called for ice-cream and
fruit afterward.   And all the time they consulted over their Christmas work, which made
it wonderfully relishing.   It was curious to
see how other people too were evidently
thinking of Christmas.   Here there was a
brown paper parcel; there somebody had an
armful; crowds came to get their luncheon or
dinner, as Norton and Matilda were doing;
stowed their packages on the chair or sofa
beside them and refitted themselves for more

shop-going. All sorts of people, — and all sorts of lunches! Some had soup and steak and tartlets; some had coffee and muffins; some had oysters and ale ; some took cups of tea and an omelet. It was as good to see what was going on, as to take her own part in it, almost, to Matilda; and yet her own part was very satisfactory. They went home only to order the horses and go to drive in the Park; Norton and she alone. It was a long afternoon of enchantment. The place, and the people, and the horses and the equipages ; and the strange animals; and the lake and its boats; everything was a delight, and Norton had as much pleasure as he expected in seeing Matilda's enjoyment and answering her questions.

" Norton," said the little girl at length, " I don't believe anybody here is having such a good time as we are."

" Why ? " said Norton.

" They don't look so."

" You can't tell about people from their looks."

" Can't you ? But I am sure you can, Norton, partly. People don't look stupid when they feel bright, do they ? "

Norton laughed a good deal at this. " But then, Pink," he remarked, " you must remember people are used to it. You have never seen it before, you know, and it's all fresh and new. It's an old story to them."

" Does everything grow to be an old story ? " said Matilda rather thoughtfully.

" I suppose so," said Norton. " That makes people always hunting up new things."

Matilda wondered silently whether it was indeed so with *everything*. Would her new dresses come to be an old story too, and she lose her pleasure in them ? Could the Park ? could the flowers ?

" Norton," she broke out, " there are *some* things that never grow to be an old story. Flowers don't."

" Flowers — no, they don't," said Norton; " that's a fact. But then, they're always new, Pink. They don't last. They are always coming up new ; that's the beauty of them."

"I do not think *that* is the beauty of them," Matilda answered slowly.

" Well, you'd get tired of them if they didn't," said Norton.

" Do people get tired of coming here ? " Matilda asked again, as her eye roved over the gay procession of carriages which just then they could trace along several turns in the road before them.

" I suppose so," said Norton. " Why not ? "

" I do not see how they ever could. Why it's beautiful, Norton ! And the air is so sweet."

" I never know how the air is."

" Don't you ! But then you lose a great deal that I don't lose. I am smelling it all the while. Are there any flowers here in summer time ? "

" Lots."

" It must be lovely then.   Norton, it must
be nice to come here and walk."

" Walking is stupid," said Norton.   " I
can't see any use in walking, except to get to
a place."

" Norton, do you see a boy yonder, coming
towards us, on a black pony ? "

" I see him."

" It looks so like David Bartholomew."

" You'll see why, in another minute.   It's
himself."

" I didn't know he rode in the Park too,"
said Matilda, as David passed them with a
bow.

" Everybody rides in the Park — or drives."

" That is what we are doing ? "

" Exactly."   ·

" I should think it was pleasant to ride on
horseback."

" This is better," said Norton.

" I wonder whether David will ever look
pleasant at me again."

" It don't signify, so far as I see," said

Norton. "David Bartholomew has his own way of looking at every thing; the Park and all. He likes to take that all alone by himself, and so he does other things. He paddles his own canoe at school, in class and out of class; he don't want help and he don't give it."

"Don't he play either, in any of your school games?"

"Yes — sometimes; but he keeps himself to himself through it all."

"Norton, do the other boys dislike him because he is a Jew?"

"No!" said Norton vehemently. "He dislikes *them* because they are not Jews; that is a nearer account of the matter. Pink, you and I are going to have lessons together."

"Does mamma say so?"

"Yes; at last; because if you went to school you would be broken off half way when we go home to Shadywalk. So mamma says we may try, and if I teach well and you learn well, she will let it stand so. How do you like it?"

" O very much, Norton! But when will you have time ?"

" I'll find the time. Now Pink, how much do you know ?"

" O Norton, you know I don't know any thing."

" That's all in the air," said Norton. " You can read, I suppose, and write ?"

" Yes, I can read and write. But then I haven't been to school in ever so long."

" Never mind that. If we go nine miles an hour, how far shall we have gone if we are out three hours and a half ? "

Matilda answered this and several more puzzling questions with pretty prompt correctness.

" You'll do," said Norton. "I knew you were sharp. You can always tell whether a person has a head, by the way he takes hold of numbers." A partial judgment, perhaps; for Norton himself was very quick at them.

" Can you read any thing except English, Pink ? " he went on.

" No, Norton."

" Never tried ? "

" No, Norton. How could I try without being taught ? "

" Of course," said Norton. " There's a jolly dog cart — isn't it ? Mamma wants you to read a lot of things besides English, I can tell you."

" How many can you read, Norton ? "

" Latin, and Greek, and German, and French, I am boring at now."

" Don't you like it ? Is it boring ? "

" I like figures better. David is great on languages. Well, Pink, you shan't have 'em all at once. Now I want to ask you another question. What do you think was the greatest battle that was ever fought in the world ? "

" Battle ? O I don't know any thing about battles, Norton."

" Well, who was the greatest hero, then; the greatest man ? "

Matilda pondered, and Norton watched her

slyly in the intervals of attending to his
ponies.

"I think, Norton, the greatest man I ever
heard about, was Moses."

Norton's face quivered with amusement,
but he kept it a little turned away from
Matilda and asked why she thought so?

"I never heard of anybody who did such
great things; nor who *had* such great things?"

"Had? What did he have?" said Norton. "I never knew he had any thing particular."

"Don't you remember? the Lord spoke
with him face to face, as we speak to each
other; and once he had a sight of that wonderful glory. It must have been something
so wonderful, Norton, for it made Moses'
face itself shine with light."

"That's a figure of speech, Pink."

"What is a figure of speech?"

"I mean, that isn't to be taken for real and
earnest, you know."

"Yes it is, Norton, for the people were

frightened when they saw him, and ran away."

" Pink, Pink, Pink!" exclaimed Norton, and stopped.

" What?" said Matilda.

" Nothing. And so Moses is your greatest man! That is all you know!"

" Why, who do you know that is greater?" said Matilda.

"You never read any history but the Bible?"

" Not much. Who do you know that is greater, Norton?"

" *Whom* do I know. Well, Pink, if I were to tell you, you wouldn't understand, till you have read about them. Why you have got all to read about. I guess you'll have to begin back with Romulus and Remus."

" How far back were they?"

" How far back? Ages; almost before history."

" Before Moses?"

" Before Moses! No, I suppose not. I

declare I don't know when that old fellow was about."

" But there is history before Moses, Norton ? "

" Not Roman history," said Norton; " and that is what we are talking about."

" Were they great, Norton ? "

" Who ? "

" Those two men you spoke of."

" Romulus and Remus? O! — Well, Romulus founded Rome."

" And when was that ? "

" Well, I don't know, that's a fact. I believe, somewhere about eight or nine centuries before our era."

" I would like to read about it," said Matilda meekly.

" And you shall," said Norton, firing up; " and there's Grecian history too, Pink; and French and English history; and German."

" And American history too ? " ventured Matilda.

" Well, yes; but you see we haven't a

great deal of history yet, Pink; because we are a young people."

" A *young* people ? " said Matilda, puzzled. " What do you mean by that ? "

" Why yes; it was only in 1776 that we set up for ourselves."

" Seventeen seventy six," repeated Matilda. " And now it is eighteen " —

" Near a hundred years; that is all."

Matilda pondered a little.

" Where must I begin, Norton ? "

" O with Romulus and Remus, I guess. And then there's grammar, Pink; did you ever study grammar ? "

" A little. I didn't like it."

" No, and I don't like it; but you have to learn it, for all that. And geography, Pink? "

" O I was drawing maps, Norton; but then I had to come away from school, and I was busy at aunt Candy's, and I have forgot nearly all I knew, I am afraid."

" Never mind," said Norton delightedly; " we'll find it again, and a great deal more.

I'll get you some nice sheets of paper for your maps, and a box of colours; so that you can make a pretty affair of them. I declare! I don't know whether we can begin, though, before Christmas."

" O yes, Norton. I have more time than I know what to do with. I would like to begin about Romus " —

" Romulus. Yes, you shall. And now, if we turn round here we shall not have too much time to get home, I'm thinking."

CHAPTER X.

MATILDA hardly knew whether to welcome Sunday. Her mind was in such a whirl, she was half afraid to have leisure to think. There was little chance however for that in the morning; late breakfast and dressing disposed of the time nicely. The whole family went to church to-day, David alone excepted; and Matilda was divided between delight in her new cloak and rich dress, and a certain troubled feeling that all the sweetness which used to belong to her Sundays in church at Shadywalk was here missing. Nothing in the service gave her any help. Her dress, to be sure, was merged in a crowd of just such dresses; silks and laces and velvets and feathers and bright colours were on every side of her · and other brilliant colours

streamed down from the painted windows of
the church. They were altogether distract-
ing. It was impossible not to notice the dash
of golden light which lay across her own
green silk dress and glorified it, so far; or to
help watching the effect of a stream of crimson rays on Judy's blue. What a purple it
made! The colouring was not any more
splendid or delicious indeed than one may
see in a summer sunset sky many a day;
but somehow the effect on the feelings was
different. And when Matilda looked up
again at the minister and tried to get at the
thread of what he was saying, she found she
had lost the connection; and began instead
to marvel how he would look, if the streak of
blue which bathed his forehead were to fall
a little lower and lie across his mouth and
chin. Altogether, when the service was
ended and the party walked home, Matilda
did not feel as if she had got any good or
refreshment out of Sunday yet; more than
out of a kaleidoscope.

" I'll go to Mr. Rush's Sunday school this afternoon " — she determined, as she was laying off her cloak.

There was no hindrance to this determination ; but as Matilda crossed the lower hall, ready to go out, she was met by Norton.

" Hollo," said he. " What's up now ? "

" Nothing is up, Norton."

" Where are you going ? "

So Matilda told him.

" Nothing else'll do, hey," said Norton. " Well, — hold on, till I get into my coat."

" Why, are *you* going ? "

" Looks like it," said Norton. " Why Pink, you are not fit to be trusted in New York streets alone."

" I know where to go, Norton. But I am very glad you will go too."

" To take care of you," said Norton. "Why Pink, New York is a big trap ; and you would find yourself at the wrong end of a puzzle before you knew it."

" I have only got two blocks more to go,

Norton. I could hardly be puzzled. Here, we turn down here."

It was no church, nor near a church, the building before which the two paused. They went up a few steps and entered a little bare vestibule. The doors giving further entrance were closed; a boy stood there as if to guard them; and a placard with a few words on it was hung up on one of them. The words were these —

"*And the door was shut.*"

"What sort of a place is this?" said Norton.

"This is the Sunday school," said Matilda. "They are singing; don't you hear them? We are late."

"It seems a queer Sunday school," said Norton. "Don't they let folks in here?"

"In ten minutes" — said the boy who stood by the door.

"Ten minutes!" echoed Norton. "It's quite an idea, to shut the door in people's faces and then hang out a sign to tell them it is shut!"

" O no, Norton;—*that* door isn't this door."

" That isn't this ? " said Norton. " What do you mean, Pink ? Of course I know so much; but it seems to me *this* is this."

" No, Norton ; it means the door spoken of in the Bible — in the New Testament;— don't you know? don't you remember?"

" Not a bit," said Norton. " I can't say, Pink, but it *seems* to me this is not just exactly the place for you to come to Sunday school. Don't look like it."

" Mr. Richmond told me to come here, you know, Norton."

But Norton looked with a disapproving eye upon what he could see of the neighbour- hood ; and it is true that nobody would have guessed it was near such a region as Bless- ington avenue. The houses were uncomely and the people were poor; and more than that. There was a look of positive want of respectability. But the little boy who was keeping the door was decent enough; and presently now he opened the door and stood by to let Norton and Matilda pass in.

There they found a large plain room, airy and roomy and light, filled with children and teachers all in a great breeze of business. Everybody seemed to be quite engrossed with something or other; and Norton and Matilda slowly went up one of the long aisles between rows of classes, waiting and looking for somebody to speak to them. The children seemed to have no eyes to give to strangers; the teachers seemed to have no time. Suddenly a young man stood in front of Norton and greeted the two very cordially.

"Are you coming to join us?" he asked with a keen glance at them. And as they did not deny it, though Norton hardly made an intelligible answer, he led them up the room and at the very top introduced them to a gentleman.

"Mr. Wharncliffe, will you take charge of these new comers? For to-day, perhaps it will be the best thing."

So Norton and Matilda found themselves at one end of a circular seat which was filled with the boys and girls of a large class. Very different from themselves these boys and girls were; belonging to another stratum of what is called society. If their dress was decent, it was as much as could be said of it; no elegance or style was within the aim of any of them; a faded frock was in one place, and a patched pair of trowsers in another place, and not one of the little company but shewed all over poverty of means and ignorance of fashion. Yet the faces testified to no poverty of wits; intelligence and interest were manifest on every one, along with the somewhat spare and pinched look of ill supplied appetites. Norton read the signs, and thought himself much out of place. Matilda read them; and shrank a little from the association. However, she reflected that this was the first day of her being in the school; doubtless when the people saw who and what she was they would put her into a class more suited to her station. Then she looked at the teacher; and she forgot her companions. He was a young man, with a very calm face and very quiet manner, whose least word and motion however was watched by the children, and his least look and gesture obeyed. He sent one of the boys to fetch a couple of Bibles for Matilda and Norton, and then bade them all open their books at the first chapter of Daniel.

The first questions were about Nebuchadnezzar and his kingdom of Babylon. Unknown subjects to most of the members of the class; Mr. Wharncliffe had to tell a great deal about ancient history and geography. He had a map, and he had a clear head of his own, for he made the talk very interesting and very easy to understand; Matilda found herself listening with much enjoyment. A question at last came to her; why the Lord gave Jehoiakim, king of Judah, into the hands of the king of Babylon? Matilda did not know. She was told to find the 25th chapter of Jeremiah and read aloud nine verses.

" Now why was it ? " said the teacher.

" Because the people would not mind the Lord's words."

The next question came to Norton. " Could the king of Babylon have taken Jerusalem, if the Lord had not given it into his hands ? "

Norton hesitated.. " I don't know, sir," he said at length.

" What do you think ? "

" I think he could."

" I should like to know why you think so."

" Because the king of Babylon was a strong king, and had plenty of soldiers and everything ; and Jehoiakim had only a little kingdom anyhow."

" The Bible says 'there is no king saved by the multitude of an host.' How do you account for the fact that when strong kings and great armies came against Jerusalem at times that she was serving and trusting God,

22

they never could do anything, but were miserably beaten ? "

" I did not know it, sir," said Norton flushing a little.

" I thought you probably did not know it," said Mr. Wharncliffe quietly. " You did not know that many a time, when the people of the Jews were following God, one man of them could chase a thousand ? "

" No, sir."

" Who remembers such a case ? "

Norton pricked up his ears and listened; for the members of the class spoke out and gave instance after instance, till the teacher stopped them for want of time to hear more. The lesson went on. The carrying away of Daniel and his companions was told of, and " the learning and the tongue of the Chaldeans " was explained. Gradually the question came round to Matilda again. Why Daniel and the other three noble young Jews would not eat of the king's meat?

Matilda could not guess.

" You remember that the Jews, as the Lord's people, were required to keep themselves ceremonially *clean*, as it was called. If they eat certain things or touched certain other things, they were not allowed to go into the temple to worship, until at least that day was ended and they had washed themselves and changed their clothes. Some-*times* many more days than one must pass before they could be 'clean' again, in that sense. This was ceremony, but it served to teach and remind them of something that was not ceremony, but deep inward truth. What ? "

Mr. Wharncliffe abruptly stopped with the question, and a tall boy at one end of the class answered him.

" People must keep themselves from what is not good."

" The people of God must keep themselves from every thing that is not pure, in word, thought, and deed. And how if they fail sometimes, Joanna, and get soiled by falling into some temptation? what must they do?"

" Get washed."

" What shall they wash in, when it is the heart and conscience that must be made clean?"

" The blood of Christ."

"How will that make us clean?"

There was hesitation in the class; then as Mr. Wharncliffe's eye came to her and rested slightly, Matilda could not help speaking.

" Because it was shed for our sins, and it takes them all away."

" *How* shall we wash in it then?" the teacher asked, still looking at Matilda.

" If we trust him?" — she began.

" To do what?"

" To forgive, — and to take away our wrong feelings."

" For his blood's sake!" said the teacher. "' They have washed their robes, and made them white in the blood of the Lamb.' And as the sacrifices of old time were a sort of picture and token of the pouring out of that blood; so the outward cleanness about which the Jews had to be so particular was a sort of sign and token of the pure heart-cleanness which every one must have who follows the Lord Jesus.

"And so we come back to Daniel. If he eat the food sent from the king's table he would be certain to touch and eat now and then something which would be, for him, cere-monially unclean. More than that. Often the king's meat was prepared from part of an animal which had been sacrificed to an idol; to eat of the sacrifice was part of the wor-ship of the idol; and so Daniel and his fellows might have been thought to share in that worship."

"But it wouldn't have been true," said a boy in the class.

"What would not have been true?"

"He would not have been worshipping the idol. He didn't mean it."

" So you think he might just as well have eaten the idol's meat? not meaning any thing."

" It wouldn't have been service of the idol."

" What would it have been ? "

" Why, nothing at all. I don't see as he would have done no harm."

" What harm would it have been, or what harm would it have done, if Daniel had *really* joined in the worship of Nebuchadnezzar's idol ? "

" He would have displeased God," said one.

" I guess God would have punished him," said another.

" He would not have been God's child any longer," said Matilda.

" All true. But is no other harm done when a child of God forgets his Father's commands? "

" He helps others to do wrong," said Matilda softly.

" He makes them think 'tain't no odds about the commands," a girl remarked.

" How's they to know what the commands is?" a second boy asked, "if he don't shew 'em ?"

" Very true, Robert," said Mr. Wharncliffe. " I have heard it said, that Christians are the only Bible some folks ever read."

" 'Cause they hain't got none ?" asked one of the class.

" Perhaps. Or if they have got one, they do not study it. But a true, beautiful life they cannot help reading; and it tells them what they ought to be."

" Daniel gave a good example," said the slim lad at the end of the class.

" That we can all do, if we have a mind, Peter. But in that case we must not *seem* to do what we ought not to do really. We help the devil that way. Now read the 9th and 10th verses. What was Daniel's friend afraid of?"

" Afraid the king would not like it."

" If Daniel and his friends did not eat like the others. Do our friends sometimes object to *our* doing right, on the ground that we shall not be like other people if we do?"

There was a general chorus of assent.

"Well, we don't want to be unlike other people, do we?"

Some said yes, and some said no; conflicting opinions.

"You say no, Heath; give us your reasons."

"They make fun of you"— said the boy, a little under breath.

"They fight you"— said another more boldly.

"They don't want to have nothing to do with you," a girl said.

"Laugh, and quarrel, and separate you from their company," repeated the teacher. "Not very pleasant things. But some of you said yes. Give us *your* reasons, if you please."

"We can't be like Christ and like the world," Peter answered.

"'Ye are not of the world, even as I am not

of the world,' " said Mr. Wharncliffe. " Most true! And some of us do want to be like our Master. Well? who else has a reason?"

" I think it is very hard," said Matilda, " to do right and not be unlike other people."

" So hard, my dear, that it is impossible," said the teacher, looking somewhat steadily at his new scholar. " And are you one of those who want to do right?"

Matilda answered; but as she did so something made her voice tremble and her eyes fill.

" For the sake of doing right, then, and for the sake of being like Jesus, some of us are willing to be unlike other people; though the consequences of that are not always pleasant. Is there nothing more to be said on the subject?"

" The people that have the Lord's name in their foreheads, will be with him by and by," remarked a girl who had not yet spoken.

" And he is with them now," said Mr. Wharncliffe. " Yes, Sarah."

" And then there will be a great gulf between," said a boy.

" Well, I think we have got reason enough," said Mr. Wharncliffe. " To be on the right side of the dividing gulf *then*, we must be content to be on the same side of it now. Daniel judged so, it is clear. On the whole, did he lose anything ? "

The teacher's eyes were looking at Norton, and he was constrained to answer no.

" What did he gain ? "

Norton was still the one looked at, and he fidgeted. Mr. Wharncliffe waited.

" I suppose, God gave him learning and wisdom."

" In consequence of his learning and wisdom, which were very remarkable, what then ? "

" The king's favour," said Norton.

" Just what the friends of the young Jews had been afraid they would lose. They ' stood before the king ; ' that means they were appointed to be king's officers ; they served him, not any meaner man. Now how does this all come home to us? How are we tempted, as Daniel and his fellows were tempted?"

Norton, at whom Mr. Wharncliffe glanced, replied that he did not know. Matilda also was silent, though longing to utter her confession. The questioning eyes passed on.

"The fellows think you must do as they does," said a lad who sat next Matilda.

"In what?"

That boy hesitated; the next spoke up, and said, "Lying, and lifting."

"And swearing," added a third.

"How if you do *not* follow their ways?"

"Some thinks you won't never get along, nohow."

"What is your opinion, Lawrence?"

The boy shifted his position a little uneasily. "They *say* you won't, teacher."

"So Daniel's friend was afraid *he* would not get along, if he did not eat the king's meat. Girls, does the temptation come to you?"

There was a general chorus of "Yes, sir," and "Yes, sir."

"Have you tried following the Lord's word against people's opinion?"

Again "Yes, sir" — came modestly from several lips.

"Do you find any ill come from it?"

"Yes, sir, a little," said a girl who might have been two or three years older than Matilda. "You get made game of, and scolded, sometimes. And they say you are lofty, or mean. Sometimes they say one to me, and sometimes the other."

"And they plague a feller," said a boy; "the worst kind."

"Is it hard to bear?"

"I think it *is*," said the girl; and one or two of the boys said again, "Yes, sir."

"Reckon you'd think so, if you tried, teacher," another put in. "They rolled Sam in the mud, the other day. There was six of 'em, you see, and he hadn't no chance."

"Sam, how did it feel? And how did you feel?"

" Teacher, 'twarn't easy to feel right."

" Could you manage it ? "

" I guess not, at first.   But afterwards I remembered."

" What did you remember ? "

" I remembered they didn't know no better, sir."

" I think you are mistaken.   They knew they were doing wrong; *how* wrong, I suppose they did not know.   Well, Sam—'if any man suffer as a Christian, let him not be ashamed, but let him glorify God on this behalf.'   Were you ashamed ? "

" No, sir."

" God says, ' Them that honour me, I will honour;' and, —' Be thou faithful unto death, and I will give thee a crown of life.'   The honour that he gives will be real honour.   It is worth while waiting for it.   Now our time will be up in two minutes — Peter, what lesson do you get from all this? for yourself? "

" To be more careful, sir."

" Of what, my boy ? "

" Careful not to have anything to do with bad ways."

" Can't be too careful; the temptation comes strong.   Ellen, what is *your* lesson ? "

" I never saw before how much a good example is."

" Ay.   God often is pleased to make it very much.   Well, Dick."

" Teacher, I don't think New York is like that 'ere place."

" Don't you ?   Why not ? "

" Folks can't get along that way in *our* streets."

" How do you find it, Sam ? and what is your conclusion from the lesson."

" I wish I was more like Dan'l, teacher."

" So I wish.   You and I are agreed, Sam. And Daniel's God is ours, remember. Heath ? "

" They was rum fellers, teacher, them 'ere."

" That is your conclusion.   Well! so some people thought then.   But Daniel and his fellows came to glory. What have you to say, Joanna?

" I think I hain't been keerful enough, teacher."

" Robert ? "

" I think it is best to let go everything else and trust God."

" You'll make no mistake so, my boy. Sarah, what is the lesson to you ? "

The girl, a very poorly dressed one, hesitated, and then said a little falteringly, —

" It's nice to be clean inside, teacher."

The teacher paused a moment also before his eye came to Matilda, and then it was very soft.

" What does my new scholar say ? "

Matilda struggled with herself, looked down and looked up, and met the kind eyes again.

" One must be willing to be unlike the world," she said.

" Is it easy ? "

" I think it is very hard, sir."

" Do you find it so, my friend ? " he asked,

his eye going on to Norton. But the bell rang just then; and in the bustle of rising and finding the hymn Norton contrived to escape the answering and yet without being rude.

As they were turning away, after the services were ended, Matilda felt a light touch on her shoulder and her teacher said quietly, "Wait." She stood still, while he went up to speak to somebody. All the other children passed out, and she was quite alone when Mr. Wharncliffe came back to her.

"Which way are you going?"

"Down the avenue, sir."

"What avenue?"

"Blessington avenue. But only to 40th street."

"Let us go together."

They had the walk to themselves; for though Norton had waited for Matilda till she came out, he sheered off when he saw what company she was in, and contented himself with keeping her in sight. Just then

Norton did not care to come to closer quarters with Mr. Wharncliffe. This gentleman talked pleasantly with Matilda; asked how she happened to come to the school, how long she had been in the city, and something about her life at Shadywalk. At last he came back to the subject of the afternoon's lesson.

" You think it is difficult to be as loyal as Daniel was ? "

" What is ' loyal,' sir ? "

" It is being a true subject, in heart; — faithful to the honour and will of one's king."

" I think it is difficult " — Matilda said in a subdued tone.

" How come you to find it so ? "

" Mr. Wharncliffe," said Matilda suddenly making up her mind, " it is very hard not to want to be fashionable."

" I don't know that there is any harm in being fashionable," said her teacher quietly. But though his face was quiet, it was so strong and good that Matilda felt great reliance on all it said.

23

" Isn't there ? " she asked quite eagerly.

" Why should there be ? "

" But — it costs so much ! " Matilda could not help confessing it.

" To be fashionable ? "

" Yes, sir."

" You do not dress yourself, I suppose. The money is not your money, is it ? "

" Yes, sir, some of it is my money ; because I have an allowance, and get my own shoes and gloves."

" And you find it costs a great deal to be fashionable ? "

" Yes, sir ; a *great* deal."

" What would you like to do with your money ? "

" There is a great deal to do," said Matilda soberly. " A great many people want help, don't they ? "

" More than you think. I could tell you of several in the class you have just been with."

" Then, sir, what ought I to do?" — and

Matilda lifted two earnest, troubled eyes to the face of her teacher.

" I think you ought to look carefully to see what the Lord has given you to do, and ask him to shew you."

" But about spending my money ? "

" Then you will better be able to tell. When you see clearly what you can do with a dollar, it will not be very hard to find out whether Jesus means you should do that with it, or buy a pair of gloves, for instance. We will talk more about this and I will help you. Here is your house. Good bye."

" But Mr. Wharncliffe," said Matilda, eagerly, as she met the clasp of his hand, — " one thing; I want to stay in your class. May I?"

" I shall be very glad to have you. Good bye."

He went off down the avenue, and Matilda stood looking after him. He was a young man ; he was hardly what people call a handsome man ; his figure had nothing imposing ; but the child's heart went after him down the

avenue.   His face had so much of the strength
and the sweetness and the beauty of goodness, that it attracted inevitably those who
saw it ; there was a look of self-poise and
calm which as surely invited trust ; truth and
power were in the face, to such a degree that
it is not wonderful a child's heart, or an older
person's, for that matter, should be won and
his confidence given even on a very short
acquaintance.   Matilda stood still in the
street, following the teacher's receding figure
with her eye.

" What are you looking at ? " said Norton,
now coming up.

" O Norton ! didn't you like the school very
much ? "

" They're a queer set," said Norton.
" They're a *poor* set, Pink ! a miserable poor
set."

" Well, what then ? Don't you like the
teacher ? "

" He's well enough ; but I don't like the
company."

" They were very well behaved, Norton;
quite as well as the children at Shadywalk."

" Shadywalk was Shadywalk," said Norton, " but here it is another thing. It won't
do. Why Pink, I shouldn't wonder if some
of them were street boys."

" I think some of those in the class were
good, Norton; boys and girls too."

" Maybe so," said Norton; " but their
clothes weren't. Faugh ! "

Matilda went into the house, wondering
at her old problem, but soon forgetting wonder in mixed sorrow and joy. All the beauty
of being a true child of God rose up fresh
before her eyes; some of the honour and
dignity of it; nothing in all the world, Matilda was sure, could be so lovely or so happy.
But she had not honoured her King like
Daniel; and that grieved her. She was very
sure now what she wanted to be.

The next morning she took up the matter
of her Christmas gifts in a new spirit. What
was she meant to do with her twenty dollars ?

Before she could decide that, she must know
a little better what it was possible to do ; and
for that Mr. Wharncliffe had promised his
help.   She must wait.   In the meanwhile she
studied carefully the question, what it was
best for her to give to her sisters and the
members of her immediate family circle ; and
very grave became Matilda's consideration of
the shops.   Her little face was almost comical now and then in its absorbed pondering
of articles and prices and calculation of sums.
An incredible number and variety of the
latter, both in addition and subtraction, were
done in her head those days, resolving twenty
dollars into an unheard of number of parts
and forming an unknown number of combi-
nations with them.   She bought the bronze
obelisk for Mrs. Laval ; partly that she might
have some pennies on hand for the street
sweepers ; but then came a time of fair
weather days, and the street sweepers were
not at the crossings.   Matilda purchased
furthermore some dark brown silk braid for

Norton's watchguard, and was happy making it, whenever she could be shut up in her room. She dared not trust Judy's eyes or tongue.

One day she was busy at this, her fingers flying over the braid and her thoughts as busy, when somebody tried to open her door, and then tapped at it. Matilda hid her work and opened, to let in Judy. She was a good deal surprised, for she had not been so honoured before. Judith and her brother were very cool and distant since the purchase of the liqueur stand.

" What do you keep your door locked for ? " was the young lady's salutation now, while her eyes roved over all the furniture and filling of Matilda's apartment.

" I was busy."

" Didn't you want anybody to come in ? "

" Not without my knowing it."

" What were you doing then ? "

" If I had wanted everybody to know, I should not have shut myself up."

" No, I suppose not. I suppose you want me out of the way, too. Well, I am not going."

" I do not want you to go, Judy, if you like to stay. That is, if you will be good."

" Good ? " said the other, her eyes snapping. " What do you call good ? "

" Everybody knows what good means, don't they ? " said Matilda.

" *I* don't," said Judy. " I have my way of being good — that's all. Everybody has his own way. What is yours ? "

" But there is only one real way."

" Ain't there, though ! " exclaimed Judy. " I'll shew you a dozen."

" They can't be all *good*, Judy."

" Who's to say they are not ? "

" Why, the Bible." The minute she had said it the colour flushed to Matilda's face. But Judy went on with the greatest coolness.

" Your Bible, or my Bible ? "

" There isn't but one Bible, Judy, that I know."

" Yes, there is ! " said the young lady fiercely. " There's our Bible, that's the true. There's yours, that's nothing, that you dare bind up with it."

" They both say the same thing," said Matilda.

" They DON'T ! " said the girl, sitting upright, and her eyes darted fire. " They don't say a word alike; don't you dare say it."

" Why Judy, what the one says is good, the other says is good; there is no difference in that. Did you ever read the New Testament ? "

" No ! and I don't want to ; nor the other either. But I didn't come to talk about that."

" What do *you* call goodness, then ? "

" Goodness ? " said Judy, relapsing into comparatively harmless mischief; " goodness? It's a sweet apple — and I hate sweet apples."

" What do you mean ? "

"I mean *that*. Goody folks are stupid. Aren't they, though!"

"But then, what is your notion of *real* goodness?"

"I don't believe there is such a thing. Come! you don't either."

"I don't believe in goodness?"

"Goodness!" repeated Judy impatiently, "you needn't stare. I don't choose to be stared at. You know it as well as I. When you are what you call good, you just want the name of it. So do I sometimes; and then I get it. That's cheap work."

"Want the name of what?"

"Why, of being good."

"Then goodness *is* something. You wouldn't want the name of nothing."

Judy laughed. "I haven't come here to be good to-day," she said; "nor to talk nonsense. I want to tell you about something. We are going to have a party."

"A party! when?"

"Christmas eve. Now it is *our* party,

you understand; mine and Norton's and David's; mamma has nothing to do with it, nor grandmamma, except to prepare everything. *That* she'll do; but we have got to prepare the entertainment; and we are going to play games and act proverbs; and I have come to see how much you know, and whether you can help."

"What do you want me to know?" said Matilda. "I'll help all I can."

"How much do you know about games? Can you play 'What's my thought like?' or 'Consequences?' or anything?"

"I never played games much," said Matilda, with a sudden feeling of inferiority. "I never had much chance."

"I dare say!" said Judy. "I knew that before I came. Well of course you can't act proverbs. You don't know anything."

"What is it?" said Matilda. "Tell me. Perhaps I can learn."

"You can't learn in a minute," said Judy with a slight toss of her head, which indeed was much given to wagging in various directions.

" But tell me, please."

" Well, there's no harm in that. We choose a proverb, of course, first; for instance the boys are going to play ' It's ill talking between a full man and a fasting.' This is how they are going to do it. Nobody knows, you understand, what the proverb is, but they must guess it. Norton will be a rich man who wants to buy a piece of land; and David is the man who owns the land and has come to see him; but he has come a good way, and he is without his dinner, and he feels as cross as can be, and no terms will suit him. So they talk and talk, and disagree and quarrel and are ridiculous; till at last Norton finds out that Davy hasn't dined; and then he orders up everything in the house he can think of, that is good, and makes him eat; and when he has eaten everything and drunk wine and they are cracking nuts, then Norton begins again about the piece of land; and the

poor man is so comfortable now he is willing
to sell anything he has got; and Norton gets
it for his own price. Won't it be good? "

" I should think it would be very interesting," said Matilda; whom indeed the description interested mightily. " But how could I
help ? I don't see."

" O not in that you couldn't, of course ;
Davy and Norton don't want any help, I
guess, from anybody ; they know all about it.
But I want you to help *me*. I wonder if you
can. I don't believe you can, either. I shall
have to get somebody else."

" What do you want me to do ? " said
Matilda, feeling socially very small indeed.

" I am going to play ' Riches bring care.'
I am a rich old woman, like grandmamma,
only not like her, for she is never worried
about anything; but I am worried to death
for fear this or that will come to harm. And
I want you to be my maid. I must have
somebody, you know, to talk to and worry
with."

"If that is all," said Matilda, "I should think I could be talked to."

"But it *isn't* all, stupid!" said Judy. "You must know how to answer back, and try to make me believe things are going right, and so worry me more and more."

"Suppose we try," said Matilda. "I don't know how I could do, but maybe I might learn."

"I'd rather have it all in the house," said Judy, "if I can. Two proverbs will be enough; for they take a good while — dressing and all, you know."

"Dressing for the proverbs?"

"Of course! Dressing, indeed! Do I look like an old woman *without* dressing? Not just yet. We must be dressed up to the work. But we can practise without being dressed. When the boys come home to-night, we'll come up here to the lobby and practise. But I don't believe you'll do."

"Will it be a large party, Judy?"

"Hm — I don't know. I guess not. Grandmamma doesn't like large parties. I dare say she won't have more than fifty."

Fifty seemed a very large party to Matilda; but she would not expose her ignorance, and so held her peace. Judy pottered about the room for a while longer, looking at everything in it, and out of it, Matilda thought; for she lounged at the windows with her arms on the sill, gazing up and down at all that was going on in the street. Finally said they would try a practice in the evening, and she departed.

CHAPTER XI.

THE acted proverbs that night went pretty well; so the boys said; and Matilda went to bed feeling that life was very delightful where such rare diversions were to be had, and such fine accomplishments acquired. The next time, Judy said, they would dress for the acting; that needed practising too.

The day following, when she got up, Matilda was astonished to find the air thick with snow and her window sills quite filled up with it already. She had meant to take a walk down town to make a purchase she had determined on; and her first thought was, how bad the walking would be now, after the dry clean streets they had rejoiced in for a week or two past. The next thought was, that the street sweepers would be out. For some time she had not seen them. They would be out in force to-day. Matilda had pennies ready; she was quite determined on the propriety of that; and she thought besides that a kind word or two might be given where she had a chance. " I am sure Jesus would speak to them," she said to herself. " He would try to do them good. I wonder, can I? But I can *try*."

She had the opportunity even sooner than she expected; for while she was eating her breakfast the snow stopped and the sun came out. So about eleven o'clock she made ready and set forth. There was a very convenient little pocket on the outside of her grey pelisse, in which she could bestow her pennies. Matilda put eleven coppers there, all she had, and one silver dime. What she was to do with that she did not know; but she thought she would have it ready.

Clear, bright and beautiful, the day was; not cold; and the city all for the moment whitened by the new fall of snow. So she

24

thought at first; but Matilda soon found there
was no whitening New York. The roadway
was cut up and dirty, of course; and the
multitudes of feet abroad dragged the dirt
upon the sidewalks. However, the sky was
blue; and defilement could not reach the sunlight; so she went along happy. But before
she got to Fourteenth Street, nine of her
eleven pennies were gone. Some timid
words had gone with them too, sometimes;
and Matilda had seen the look of dull asking
change to surprise and take on a gleam of
life in more than one instance; that was all
that could be said. Two boys had assured
her they went to Sunday school; one or two
others of whom she had asked the question
had not seemed to understand her. Had it
done any good? She could not tell; how
could she tell? Perhaps her look and her
words and her penny, all together, might have
brought a bit of cheer into lives as much
trampled into the dirt as the very snow they
swept. Perhaps; and *that* was worth work-

ing for; "anyhow, all I can do, is all I can do," thought Matilda. She mused too on the swift way money has of disappearing in New York. Norton's watchguard had cost twenty eight cents; the obelisk, two dollars; now the dress she was on her way to buy for Letitia would take two dollars and a half more; there was already almost five gone of her twenty. And of even her pennies she had only two left, with the silver bit. "However, they won't expect me to give them anything *again* as I go back," she thought, referring to the street sweepers. "Once in one morning will do, I suppose."

Just as she said this to herself, she had come to another crossing, a very busy one, where carts and carriages were incessantly turning down or coming up; keeping the sweeper in work. It was a girl this time; as old or older than herself; a little tidy, with a grim old shawl tied round her waist and shoulders, but bare feet in the snow. Matilda might have crossed in the crowd without meeting her, but she waited to speak and give her penny. The girl's face encouraged her.

" Are you not very cold ? " Matilda asked.

" No — I don't think of it." The answer seemed to come doubtfully.

" Do you go to Sunday school anywhere ? "

The girl sprang from her at this minute to clear the way for some dainty steppers, where the muddy snow had been flung by the horses' feet just a moment before; and to hold her hand for the penny, which was not given. Slowly she came back to Matilda.

" Do most of the people give you something ? "

" No," said the girl. " Most of 'em don't."

" Do you go to Sunday school on Sundays ? "

" O yes: I go to Mr. Rush's Sunday school, in Forty Second street."

" Why, *I* go there," said Matilda. " Who's your teacher ? "

The girl's face quite changed as she now

looked at her; it grew into a sort of answering sympathy of humanity; there was almost a dawning smile.

"I remember you," she said; "I didn't at first, but I do now. You were in the class last Sunday. I am in Mr. Wharncliffe's class."

"Why so do I remember you!" cried Matilda. "You are Sarah?"

The conversation was interrupted again, for the little street-sweeper was neglecting her duties, and she ran to attend to them. Out and in among the carriages and horses' feet. Matilda wondered why she did not get thrown down and trampled upon; but she was skilful and seemed to have eyes in the back of her head, for she constantly kept just out of danger. Matilda waited to say a little more to her, for the talk had become interesting; in vain, the little street-sweeper was too busy, and the morning was going; Matilda had to attend to her own business and be home by one o'clock. She had found, she

thought, the place where her silver dime belonged; so she dropped it into Sarah's hand
as she passed, with a smile, and went on her
way. This time she got an unmistakable
smile in return, and it made her glad.

So she was in a class with a street-
sweeper! Matilda reflected as she went on
down Broadway. Well, what of it? They
would think it very odd at home! And somehow it seemed odd to Matilda herself. Had
she got a little out of her place in going to
Mr. Rush's Sunday school? Could it be best
that such elegant robes, made by Mme. Fournissons, should sit in the same seat with a
little street girl's brown rags? " She was not
ragged on Sunday, though," thought Matilda;
" poor enough; and some of those boys were
street boys, I dare say. However, Mr. Wharncliffe is a gentleman; there is no doubt of
that; and he likes his class; some of them are
good, I think. And if they are, Jesus loves
them. He loves them whether or no. How
odd it is that we don't!" —

Matilda went on trying to remember all that Sarah had said in the school; but the different speakers and words were all jumbled up in her mind, and she could not quite separate them. She forgot Sarah then in the delightful business of choosing a dress for Letitia; a business so difficult withal that it was like to last a long time, if Matilda had not remembered one o'clock. She feared she would be late; yet a single minute more of talk with the street girl she must have; she walked up to Fourteenth street. Sarah was there yet, busy at her post. She had a smile again for Matilda.

" Are you not tired?" the rich child asked of the poor one.

"I don't think of being tired," was the answer.

" What time do you go home to dinner?"

" Dinner?" said Sarah; and she shook her head. " I don't go home till night. I can't."

" But how do you take your dinner?" Matilda asked.

The girl flushed a little, and hesitated. " I can take it here," she said.

" Standing ? and in this crowd ? "

"No. — I go and sit down somewheres. 'Tain't such a dinner as you have. It's easy took."

" Sarah," said Matilda suddenly, " you love Jesus, don't you ?"

" Who ?" she said, for the noise and rush of horses and carriages in the streets was tremendous, and the children both sprang back to the sidewalk just then out of the way of something. "Jesus? Was it *that* you asked?"

She stood leaning on her broom and looking at her questioner. Matilda could see better now how thin the face was, how marked with care; but at the same time a light came into it like a sunbeam on a winter landscape; the grey changed to golden somehow; and the set of the girl's lips, gentle and glad, was very sweet.

"Do I love him?" she repeated. " He is with me here all the day when I am sweeping the snow. Yes, I love him! and he loves me. That is how I live."

"That's how I want to live too," said Matilda; "but sometimes I forget."

"I shouldn't think *you'd* forget," said Sarah. "It must be easy for you."

"What must be easy?"

"I should think it would be easy to be good," said the poor girl, her eye going unconsciously up and down over the tokens of Matilda's comfortable condition.

"I don't think having things helps one to be good," said Matilda. "It makes it hard, sometimes."

"I sometimes think *not* having things makes it hard," said the other, a little wistfully. "But Jesus is good, anyhow!" she added with a content of face which was unshadowed.

"Good bye," said Matilda. "I shall see you again." And she ran off to get into a horse car. The little street-sweeper stood and looked after her. There was not a thing that the one had but the other had it not. She looked, and turned to her sweeping again.

Matilda on her part hurried along, with a heart quite full, but remembering at the same time that she would be late at lunch. At the corner where she stopped to wait for a car there was a fruit stall, stocked with oranges, apples, candies and gingerbread. It brought back a thought which had filled her head a few minutes ago; but she was afraid she would be late. She glanced down the line of rails to the car seen coming in the distance, balanced probabilities a moment, then turned to the fruit woman. She bought a cake of gingerbread and an orange and an apple; had to wait what seemed a long time to receive her change; then rushed across the block to where she had left Sarah, stopped only to put the things in her hands, and rushed back again; not in time to catch her car, which was going on merrily out of her hail. But the next one was not far behind;

and Matilda enjoyed Sarah's lunch all the way to her own.

" But this is only for one day. And there are so many days, and so many people that want things. I must save every bit of money I can."

She was late; but she was so happy and hungry, that her elders looked on her very indulgently, it being, as in truth she was, a pleasant sight.

That evening Judith proposed another practising of the proverb she and Matilda were to act together; and this time she dressed up for it. A robe of her mother's, which trailed ridiculously over the floor; jewels of value in her ears and on her hands and neck; and finally a lace scarf of Mrs. Lloyd's, which was very rich and extremely costly. Norton was absent on some business of his own; David was the only critic on hand. He objected.

" You can act just as well without all that trumpery, Judith."

" Trumpery! That's what it is to you. My shawl is worth five hundred dollars if it is worth a dollar. It is worth a great deal more than that, I believe; but I declare I get confused among the prices of things. That is one of the cares of riches, that try me most."

" You can act just as well without all that, Judy."

" I can't!"

" You can just as well, if you would only think so."

" Very likely; but I don't think so; that just makes it, you see. I want to feel that I am rich; how am I going to get the idea in my head, boy? — I declare, Satinalia, I think this satin dress is getting frayed already."

" How ought I to be dressed?" inquired Matilda.

" O just as you are. You haven't to make believe, you know; you have got only to act yourself. Come, begin. — I declare, Satinalia, I think this satin dress is getting frayed already."

Matilda hesitated, then put by the displeasure which rose at Judy's rudeness, and entered into the play.

" And how shouldn't it, ma'am, when it's dragging and streaming all over the floor for yards behind you. Satin won't bear every thing."

" No, the satin one gets now-a-days won't. I could buy satin once, that would wear out two of this; and this cost five dollars a yard. Dear me! I shall be a poor woman yet."

" If you were to cut off the train, ma'am, the dress wouldn't drag so."

" Wouldn't it! you Irish stupid. O I hear something breaking downstairs! Robert has smashed a tray-ful, I'll be bound. I heard the breaking of glass. Run, Satinalia, run down as hard as you can and find out what it is. Run before he gets the pieces picked up; for then I shall never know what has happened."

" You'd miss the broken things," said Matilda; not exactly as Satinalia.

" You're an impudent hussy, to answer me

so. Run and see what it is, I tell you, or I shall never know."

" What must I say it is?" said Matilda, out of character.

"Haven't you wit enough for that?" said Judith, also speaking in her own proper. "Say any thing you have a mind; but don't stand poking there. La! you haven't seen any thing in all your life, except a liqueur stand. Say any thing! and be quick."

Matilda ran down a few stairs, and paused, not quite certain whether she would go back. She was angry. But she wanted to be friends with Judy and her brother; and the thought of her motto came to her help. "Do all in the name of the Lord Jesus;" — then certainly with courtesy and patience and kindness, as his servant should. She prayed for a kind spirit, and went back again.

" You've been five ages," cried the rich woman. " Well, what's broke?"

" Ma'am, Robert has let fall a tray full of claret glasses, and the salad dish with a pointed edge."

" *That* salad dish ! " exclaimed Judy. " It was the richest in New York. The Queen of England had one like it; and nobody else but me in this country. I told Robert to keep it carefully done up in cotton; and *never* to wash it. That is what it is to have things."

" Don't it have to be washed ? " inquired Matilda.

" I wish I could get into your head," said Judy impatiently and speaking quite as Judy, " that you are a maid servant and have no business to ask questions. I suppose you never knew anything about maid-servants till you came here; but you have been here long enough to learn *that,* if you were not perfectly *bourgeoise !* "

" Hush, Judy; you forget yourself," said David.

" She don't understand ! " said the polite young lady.

" You do not get on with your proverb at this rate," he went·on, glancing at Ma-

tilda, whose cheek gave token of some understanding.

" Stupid!" said Judy, returning to her
charge and play, — "don't you understand
that when that dish is used I wash it myself?
And what claret glasses were they? I'll be
bound they are the yellow set with my
crest?"

" Those are the ones," Satinalia assented.

" That is what it is to have things! My
life is one trouble. Satinalia!" —

" Ma'am."

" I haven't got my diamond bracelet on."

" No, ma'am; I do not see it." .

" Well, go and see it. Find it and bring
it to me. I want it on with this dress."

Matilda being instructed in this part of
her duties, reported that she could not find
the bracelet. The jewel box was ordered in,
and examined, with a great many lamenta-
tions and conjectures as to the missing
article. Finally the supposed owner declared
she must write immediately to her jewellers

to know if they had the bracelet, either for repair or safe keeping. Satinalia was despatched for a writing desk; and then for a candle.

" There are no tapers in this concern," Judy remarked; " and the note must be sealed. Somebody might find out that the bracelet is missing, and so it would be missing for ever, from me. Satinalia, what do you stand there for? Do you not hear me say I want a candle?"

" Can't you make believe as well?" asked Matilda, not Satinalia.

" You are too tiresome!" exclaimed Judy. " What do you know about it, at all, I should like to know. I think, when I give you the favour of playing with me, that is enough. You do as I tell you."

Matilda went for the candle, inwardly resolving that she would not enjoy the privilege of practising with Judy another time unless Norton were by. In his presence she was protected. A tear or two came from

25

the little girl's eyes, before she got back to the lobby with the lighted candle. Judy perhaps wanted to make a tableau of herself at the letter sealing; for she took an elegant attitude, that threw her satin drapery imposingly about her and displayed her bare arm somewhat theatrically, gleaming with jewels and softened by the delicate lace of the scarf. But thereby came trouble. In a careless sweep of her arm, sealing-wax in hand, no doubt intended to be very graceful, the lace came in contact with the flame of the candle; and a hole was burnt in the precious fabric before anybody could do any thing to prevent it. Then there was dismay. Judy shrieked and flung herself down with her head on her arms. David and Matilda looked at the lace damage, and looked at each other. Even he looked grave.

"It's a pretty bad business," he concluded.

"O what shall I do! O what shall I do!" Judith cried. "O what *will* grandmamma say! O I wish Christmas never came!" —

" What sort of lace is this?" Matilda asked, still examining the scarf which David had let fall from his fingers. He thought it an odd question and did not answer. Judy was crying and did not hear.

" The best thing is to own up now, Judy," said her brother. " It is no use to cry."

" Yes, it is!" said Judy vehemently. " That's all a boy knows about it; but they don't know everything."

" I don't *see* the use of it, at all events," said David. " If tears were spiders, they might mend it."

" Spiders mend it!" repeated Judy. " David, you are enough to provoke a saint."

" But you are not a saint," said her brother. " It need not provoke you. What are you going to do?"

" Judy," said Matilda suddenly, " look here. Does your grandmother often wear this?"

" She'll be sure to want it now," said Judy, " if she never did before."

" It doesn't help the matter either," said

David. " Putting off discovery is no comfort. I always think it is best to be out with
a thing and have done with it."

"No," said Matilda. " Yes; — that isn't
what I mean ; but I mean, will Mrs. Lloyd
want to wear this now for a few days —
four or five ? "

" She won't wear it before our party," said
Judy. " There's nothing going on or coming off before that. O I wish our party was
in Egypt."

" Then don't," said Matilda. " Look here,
— listen. I think perhaps, — I don't promise,
you know, for I am not sure, — but I think
perhaps I can mend this."

" You can't, my girl," said David, " unless
you are a witch."

" You might as well mend the house!"
said Judy impatiently. " It isn't like darning
stockings, I can tell you."

" I know how to darn stockings," said
Matilda; "and I do not mean to mend this,
that way. But I can mend some lace ; and

I think — perhaps — I can this. If you will let me, I'll try."

" How come you to think you can?" David asked. " I should say it was impossible, to anything but a fairy."

" I have been taught," said Matilda. " I did not like to learn, but I am very glad now I did. Do you like to have me try?"

" It is very kind of you," said David; " but I can't think you can manage it."

" Of course she can't!" said Judy contemptuously.

" If I only had the right thread," said Matilda, re-examining the material she had to deal with.

" What must it be?" David inquired.

" Look," said Matilda. " Very, very, *very* fine, to match this."

" Where can it be had? You are sure you will not make matters worse by doing any thing with it? Though I don't see how they could be worse, that's a fact. I'll get the thread."

So it was arranged between them, without reference to Judy.   Matilda carried the scarf to her room; and Judy ungraciously and ungracefully let her go without a word.

" You are not very civil, Judy," said her brother.

" Civil, to that creature ! "

" Civil to anybody," said David ; " and she is a very well-behaved creature, as you call her."

" She was well-behaved at Candello's the other day, wasn't she ? "

" Perhaps she was, after her fashion. Come, Judy, you have tried her to-night, and she has borne it as you wouldn't have borne it; or I either."

" She knew better than not to bear it," said Judy insolently.

" I wish you had known better than to give it her to bear.   She was not obliged to bear it, either.   Aunt Zara would not take it very well, if she was to hear it."

Judy only pouted, and then went on with

a little more crying for the matter of the shawl. David gave up his part of the business.

Except looking for the thread. That he did faithfully; but he did not know where to go to find the article and of course did not find it. What he brought to Matilda might as well have been a cable, for all the use she could make of it in the premises. There was no more to do but to tell Mrs. Laval and get her help; and this was the course finally agreed upon between Matilda and David; Judy was not consulted.

Mrs. Laval heard the story very calmly; and immediately promised to get the thread, which she did. Matilda could not also obtain from her an absolute promise of secrecy. Mrs. Laval reserved that; only assuring Matilda that she would do no harm, and that she would say nothing at least until it should be seen whether or no Matilda had succeeded in the repair of the scarf.

And now for days thereafter Matilda was

most of the time shut up in her room, with the door locked. It was necessary to keep out Judy; the work called for Matilda's whole and best attention. It was not an easy or a small undertaking. If anybody could have looked in through the closed door those days, he would have seen a little figure seated on a low foot-cushion, with a magnificent lace drapery lying over her lap and falling to the floor. On a chair at her side were her thread and needles and scissors; and very delicately and slowly Matilda's fingers were busy trying to weave again the lost meshes of the exquisite lace. They worked and worked, hour after hour, before she could be certain whether she was going to succeed; and the blood flushed into Matilda's cheeks with the excitement and the intense application. At last, Saturday afternoon, enough progress was made to let the little girl see that, as she said to herself, " it would do;" and she put the scarf away that afternoon feeling that she was all ready for Sunday to come now, and could enjoy it without a drawback of any sort.

And so she did — even Dr. Broadman and his parti-coloured church. Matilda's whole heart had turned back to its old course; that course which looks to Jesus all the way. Sunlight lies all along that way, as surely as one's face is turned to the sun; so Matilda felt very happy. She hoped, too, that she was gaining in the goodwill of her adopted cousins; David certainly had spoken and looked civilly and pleasantly again; and Matilda's heart to-day was without a cloud.

Norton declined to go with her to Sunday school, however, and she went alone. No stranger now, she took her place in the class as one at home; and all the business and talk of the hour was delightful to her. Sarah was there of course; after the school services were ended Matilda seized her opportunity.

" Whereabouts do you live, Sarah ? "

Matilda had been turning over various vague thoughts in her mind, compounded from experiences of Lilac lane and the snowy corner of Fourteenth street; her question was not without a purpose. But Sarah answered generally, that it was not very far off.

" Where is it?" said Matilda. " I should like, if I can, and maybe I can, I should like to come and see you."

" It is a poor place," said Sarah. " I don't think you would like to come into it."

" But you live there," said the other child.

" Yes" — said Sarah uneasily; " I live there when I ain't somewheres else; and I'm that mostly."

" Where is that 'somewhere else'? I'll come to see you there, if I can."

" You *have* seen me there," said the street-sweeper. " 'Most days I'm there."

" I have been past that corner a good many times, Sarah, when I couldn't see you anywhere."

" 'Cos the streets was clean. There warn't no use for my broom then. Nobody'd ha'

wanted it, or me. I'd ha' been took up,
maybe."

"What do you do *then*, Sarah?"

"Some days I does nothing; some days
I gets something to sell, and then I does
that."

"But I would like to know where you
live."

"You wouldn't like it, I guess, if you saw
it. Best not," said Sarah. "They wouldn't
let you come to such a place, and they hadn't
ought to. I'd like to see you at my crossing," she added with a smile as she moved
off. Matilda, quite lost in wonderment, stood
looking after her as she went slowly down the
aisle. Her clothes were scarcely whole, yet put
on with an evident attempt at tidiness; her
bonnet was not a bonnet, but the unshapely
and discoloured remains of what had once had
the distinction. Her dress was scarcely clean;
yet as evidently there was an effort to be as
neat as circumstances permitted. What sort
of a home could it be, where so nice a girl as

Matilda believed this one was, could reach no more actual and outward nicety in her appearance?

" You have made Sarah Staples' acquaintance, I see;" Mr. Wharncliffe's voice broke her meditations.

" I saw her at her crossing one day. Isn't she a good girl?"

" She *is* a good girl, I think. What do you think?"

" O I think so," said Matilda; " I thought so before; but — Mr. Wharncliffe — I am afraid she is very poor."

" I am not afraid so; I know it."

" She will not tell me where she lives," said Matilda rather wistfully.

" Do you want to know?"

" Yes, I wanted to know; but I think she did not want I should."

" Did you think of going to see her, that you tried to find out?"

" I would have liked to go, if I could," said Matilda, looking perplexed. " But she seemed to think I wouldn't like it, or that I ought not, or something."

"She is right," said Mr. Wharncliffe. "You would not take any pleasure in seeing Sarah's home; and you cannot go there alone. But with me you may go. I will take you there, if you choose."

"Now?"

"Yes."

"Thank you, sir. I would like it."

Truth to tell, Matilda would have liked a walk in any direction and for any purpose, in company with that quiet, pleasant, kind, strong face. She had taken a great fancy and given a great trust already to her new teacher. That walk did not lessen either. Hand in hand they went along, through poor streets and in a neighbourhood that grew more wretched as they went further; yet though Matilda was in a measure conscious of this, she seemed all the while to be walking in a sort of spotless companionship; which perhaps she was. The purity made more impression upon her than the impurity. And, withal that the part of the city they were coming to was very miserable, and more wicked than miserable, Matilda saw it through an atmosphere of very pure and sweet talk.

She drew a little closer to her guide, however, as one after another sight and sound of misery struck her senses. A knot of drunken men wrestling; single specimens, very ugly to see; voices loud and brutal coming out of drinking shops; haggard-looking, dirty women, in dismal rags or finery worse yet; crying children; scolding mothers; a population of boys and girls of all ages, who evidently knew no Sabbath, and to judge by appearances had no home; and streets and houses and doorways so squalid, so encumbered with garbage and filth, so morally distant from peace and purity, that Matilda felt as if she were walking with an angel through regions where angels never stay. Perhaps Mr. Wharncliffe noticed the tightening clasp of her fingers upon his. He paused at length; it was before a large, lofty brick building at the corner of a block. No better in its moral indications than other houses around;. this was merely one of mammoth proportions. At the corner a flight of stone steps went down to a cellar floor. Standing just at the top of these steps, Matilda could look down and partly look in; though there seemed little light below but what came from this same entrance way. The stone steps were swept. But at the bottom there was nothing but a mud floor; doubtless dry in some weathers, but at this time of encumbering snow it was stamped into mud. Also down there, in the doubtful light, Matilda discerned an overturned broken chair and a brown jug; and even caught a glimpse of the corner of a small cooking stove. People lived there! or at least cooked and eat, or perhaps sold liquor. Matilda looked up, partly in wonder, partly in dismay, to Mr. Wharncliffe's face.

" This is the place," he said; and his face

was grave enough then. " Would you like
to go in ? "

" This ? " said Matilda bewildered. " *This*
isn't the place ? She don't live *here?* Does
anybody live here ? "

" Come down and let us see. You need
not be afraid," he said. " There is no danger."

Very unwillingly Matilda let the hand that
held her draw her on to descend the steps.
If this was Sarah's home, she did not wonder at the girl's hesitation about making it
known. Sarah was quite right; it was no
place fit for Matilda to come to. How could
she help letting Sarah see by her face how
dreadful she thought it ?

Meanwhile she was going down the stone
steps. They landed her in a cellar room; it
was nothing but a cellar; and without the
clean dry paving of brick or stone which we
have in the cellars of our houses. The little
old cooking stove was nearly all the furniture;
two or three chairs or stools were around,

but not one of them whole; and in two corners were heaps, of what? Matilda could not make out anything but rags, except a token of straw in one place. There was a forlorn table besides with a few specimens of broken crockery upon it. A woman was there; very poor though not *bad*-looking; two bits of ragged boys; and lastly Sarah herself, decent and grave, as she had just come from Sunday school, sitting on a box with her lesson book in her hand. She got up quickly and came forward with a surprised face, in which there shone also that wintry gleam of pleasure that Matilda had seen in it before. The pleasure was for the sight of Mr. Wharncliffe; perhaps Sarah was shy of her other visiter. However, Mr. Wharncliffe took the conversation upon himself, and left it to nobody to feel or shew awkwardness; which both Matilda and Sarah were ready to do. He had none; Matilda thought he never could have any, anywhere; so gracious, so free, his

26

words and manner were in this wretched place; so pleasant and kind, without a trace of consciousness that he had ever been in a better room than this. And yet his boot heels made prints in the damp earth floor. The poor slatternly woman roused up a little to meet his words of cheer and look of sympathy; and Sarah came and stood by his shoulder. It was an angel's visit. Matilda saw it, as well as she knew that she had been walking with one; he brought some warmth and light even into that drear region; some brightness even into those faces; though he staid but a few minutes. Giving then a hearty hand grasp, not to his scholar only but to the poor woman her mother, whom Matilda thought it must be very disagreeable to touch, he with his new scholar came away.

Matilda's desire to talk or wish to hear talking had suddenly ended. She threaded the streets in a maze; and Mr. Wharncliffe was silent; till block after block was passed and gradually a region of comparative order and beauty was opening to them. At last he looked down at his little silent companion.

" This is a pleasanter part of the city, isn't it ? "

" O Mr. Wharncliffe ! " Matilda burst forth, " why do they live there ? "

" Because they cannot live anywhere else."

" They are so poor as that ? "

" So poor as that. And a great many other people are so poor as that."

" How much would it cost ? "

" For them to move ? Well, it would cost the rent of a better room ; and they haven't got it. The mother cannot earn much ; and Sarah is the chief stay of the family."

" Have they nothing to live upon, but the pennies she gets for sweeping the crossing ? "

" Not much else. The mother makes slops, I believe ; but that brings in only a few more coppers a week."

" How much *would* a better room cost, Mr. Wharncliffe ? "

" A dollar a week, maybe; more or less, as the case might be."

There was silence again; until Mr. Wharncliffe and Matilda had come to Blessington avenue and were walking down its clean and spacious sideway.

" Mr. Wharncliffe," said Matilda suddenly, " why are some people so rich and other people so poor? "

" There are a great many reasons."

" What are some of them? can't I understand? "

" You can understand this; that people who are industrious, and careful, and who have a talent for business, get on in the world better than those who are idle or wasteful or self-indulgent or wanting in cleverness."

" Yes; I can understand that."

" The first class of people make money, and their children, who maybe are neither careful nor clever, inherit it; along with their business friends, and their advantages and opportunities; while the children of the idle and vicious inherit not merely the poverty but to some extent the other disadvantages of their parents. So óne set are naturally growing richer and richer and the other naturally go on from poor to poorer."

" Yes, I understand *that*," said Matilda, with a perplexed look. " But some of these poor people are not bad nor idle ? "

" Perhaps their parents have been. Or without business ability ; and the one thing often leads to another."

" But " — said Matilda, and stopped.

" What is it ? "

" It puzzles me, sir. I was going to say, God could make it all better ; and why don't he ? "

" He will do everything for us, Matilda," said her friend gravely, " except those things he has given *us* to do. He will help us to do those ; but he will not prevent the consequences of our idleness or disobedience. Those we must suffer ; and others suffer with us, and because of us."

"But then "— said Matilda looking up, —"the rich ought to take care of the poor."

"That is what the Lord meant we should do. We ought to find them work, and see that they get proper pay for it; and not let them die of hunger or disease in the mean while."

"Well, why don't people do so?" said Matilda.

"Some try. But in general, people have not come yet to love their neighbours as themselves."

"Thank you, Mr. Wharncliffe," Matilda said, as he stopped at the foot of Mrs. Lloyd's steps.

He smiled, and inquired, "For what?"

"For taking me there."

"Why?" said he, growing grave.

But a little to his surprise the little girl hurried up the steps without making him any answer.

In the house, she hurried in like manner up the first flight of stairs and up the second flight. Then, reaching her own floor, where nobody was apt to be at that time of Sunday afternoons, the child stopped and stood still.

She did not even wait to open her own door; but clasping the rail of the balusters she bent down her little head there and burst into a passion of weeping. Was there such utter misery in the world, and near her, and she could not relieve it? Was it possible that another child, like herself, could be so unlike herself in all the comforts and helps and hopes of life, and no remedy? Matilda could not accept the truth which her eyes had seen. She recalled Sarah's gentle, grave face, and sober looks, as she had seen her on her crossing, along with the gleam of a smile that had come over them two or three times; and her heart almost broke. She stood still, sobbing, thinking herself quite safe and alone; so that she started fearfully when she suddenly heard a voice close by her. It was David Bartholomew, come out of his room.

"What in the world's to pay?" said he.

" What *is* the matter?   You needn't start as
if I were a grisly bear!   But what *is* the
matter, Tilly ? "

Matilda was less afraid of him lately; and
she would have answered, but there was too
much to say.   The burden of her heart could
not be put into words at first.   She only
cried aloud, —

" Oh David! — Oh David! "

" What then ? " said David.   " What has
Judy been doing ? "

" Judy!   O nothing.   I don't mind Judy."

" Very wise of you, I'm sure, and I am
very glad to hear it.   What *has* troubled
you ? something bad, I should judge."

" Something so bad, you could never think
it was true," said Matilda, making vain
efforts to dry off the tears which kept welling
freshly forth.

" Have you lost something ? "

" I ?   O no ; I haven't got any thing to
lose.   Nothing particular, I mean.   But I
have seen such a place " —

" A *place?*" said David, very much puzzled. " What about the place ? "

" Oh, David, such a place! And people
live there !" — Matilda could not get on.

David was curious. He stood and waited,
while Matilda sobbed and tried to stop and
talk to him. For, seeing that he wanted to
hear, it was a sort of satisfaction to tell to
some one what filled her heart. And at last,
being patient, he managed to get a tolerably
clear report of the case. He did not run off
at once then. He stood still looking at
Matilda.

" It's disgraceful," he said. " It didn't use
to be so among my people."

" And, oh David, what can we do ? What
can I do ? I don't feel as if I could *bear* to
think that Sarah must sleep in that place
to-night. Why the floor was just earth,
damp and wet. And not a bedstead — just
think! What can I do, David ? "

" I don't see that you can do much. You
cannot build houses to lodge all the poor of

the city. That would take a good deal of money ; more than you have got, little one."

"But — I can't reach them all, but I can do something for this one," said Matilda. "I *must* do something."

"Even that would take a good deal of money," said David.

"I must do something," Matilda repeated. And she went to her own room to ponder how, while she was getting ready for dinner. Could she save anything from her Christmas money?

CHAPTER XII.

MATILDA'S thoughts about Christmas took now another character. Instead of the delightful confusion of pretty things for rich hands, among which she had only to choose, her meditations dwelt now upon the homelier supplies of the wants of her poor little neighbour. What could be had instead of that damp cellar with its mud floor? how might some beginnings of comfort be brought to cluster round the little street-sweeper, who except in Sunday school had hardly known what comfort was? It lay upon Matilda's heart; she dreamed about it at night and thought about it nearly all day, while she was mending Mrs. Lloyd's lace shawl.

The shawl was getting mended; that was a satisfactory certainty; but it took a great deal of time. Slowly the delicate fabric seemed to grow, and the place that the candle flame had entered seemed to be less and less; very slowly, for the lace was exceedingly fine and the tracery of embroidered or wrought flowers was exceeding rich. Matilda was shut up in her room the most part of the time that week; it was the Christmas week, and the shawl must be finished before the party of Friday night. Mrs. Laval sometimes came in to look at the little worker and kiss her. And one afternoon Norton came pounding at her door.

"Is it you, Norton?"

"Of course. Come out, Pink; we want you."

Matilda put down her work and opened the door.

"Come out; we are going to rehearse, and we want you, Pink."

"I should like to come, Norton, but I can't."

"What's the mischief? Why do you whisper?"

" I am not about any mischief; but I am
busy, Norton. I cannot come, indeed."

Norton pushed himself a little way into the
room.

" Busy about what?" said he. " That's all
bosh. What are you busy about? What is
that? Hullo!"

For Norton's eye, roving round the room,
caught the rich lace drapery which lay upon
one of Matilda's chairs. He went closer to
look at it, and then turned an amazed eye
upon her.

" I know what this is, Pink. Whatever
have you got it here for?"

" Hush, Norton; I am mending it."

" *Mending* it! have you broken it?"

" No, not I; but Judy would wear it one
night when we were practising; and it got in
the flame of the candle and was burnt; and
Judy was frightened, and I thought maybe I
could mend it; and see, Norton,—you can
hardly tell the place, or you won't, when I
have finished."

Norton fairly drew a low whistle and sat down to consider the matter.

" And *this* is what keeps you away so. Judy will be obliged to you, I hope. She doesn't deserve it. And grandmamma don't know! Well, Pink, I always said you were a brick."

Matilda smiled and took up her mending.

" But how are you going to be ready for Christmas ? "

" O I think about it, Norton, while I am working."

" Yes, but thinking will not buy your things."

" *That* won't take very long. I do not think I shall get a great deal now. O Norton, I have found something else that wants money."

" Money! I dare say," said Norton. "Everything wants money. What is it, Pink? It isn't Lilac lane, anyhow."

" No, Norton ; but worse."

" Go on," said Norton. " You needn't stop and look so. *I* can stand it. What is it ? "

Matilda dropped her lace for the minute, and told her walk and visit of Sunday afternoon. As she told it, the tears gathered; and at the end she dropped her face upon her knees and sobbed. Norton did not know what to do.

" There's lots of such places," he said at last. " You needn't fret so. This isn't the only one."

" O Norton, that makes it worse. One is enough; and I cannot help that; and I *must.*"

" Must what?" said Norton. " Help them? You cannot, Pink. It is no use for you to try to lift all New York on your shoulders. It's no use to think about it."

" I am not going to try to lift all New York," said the little girl, making an effort to dry her eyes.

" And it is no good crying about it, you know."

" No, no good," said Matilda. " But I don't know, Norton; perhaps it is. If other people cried about it, the thing would get mended."

"Not so easy as lace work," said Norton, looking at the cobweb tracery tissue before him.

"But it must be mended, Norton?" said Matilda inquiringly, and almost imploringly.

"Well, Pink, anybody that tries it will get mired. That's all I have to say. There's no end to New York mud."

"But we can lift people out of it."

"*I* can't," said Norton. "Nor you neither. No, you can't. There's lots of societies and institutions and committees and boards, and all that sort of thing; and no end of collections and contributions; and the people that get the collections must attend to the people they are collected for. *We* can't, you know. Well, I must go and rehearse."

He went off; but immediately after another tap at the door announced David. He stepped inside the door; a great mark of condescension. He had never come to Matilda's room until now.

"So busy you can't spare time for prov-

erbs?" he said. "But what is the matter?"
For Norton's want of sympathy had disappointed Matilda, and she had tears in her
eyes and on her cheeks again. What should
she do now? she thought. She had half
counted on Norton's helping her. David
was quite earnest to know the cause of
trouble; and Matilda at last confessed she
was thinking about the people that lived in
that cellar room.

"Where is the place?" David inquired.

"I can't tell; and I am sure you couldn't
find it. We turned and turned, going and
coming. It's an ugly way too. You couldn't
find it, David."

"But your crying will not help them, Tilly."

"No," said Matilda, trying to dash the tears
away. "If I could help them, I wouldn't cry.
But I must. O think of living so, David!
No beds, that we would call beds; and those
on the dirty ground; and living without *anything*. O I didn't know people lived so!
What can I do?"

27

"I'll tell you," said David. "We'll try to find another place for them to live, and see how much that would cost; and then we can lay our plans."

Matilda was breathless for a minute. "O thank you. How can we find out about that? I might ask Mr. Wharncliffe! mightn't I?"

"I should think you might."

"Then I'll do that, next time I see him. But I haven't got much money, David."

"Well, we'll see about that. Find out how much a decent lodging would cost; and then we can tell, you know. I'll make Judy help; and Norton will shell out something. He always keeps holes in his purse."

"I don't see how he can have much in it, then," said Matilda, trying to laugh. "But you are *very* good, David."

"Well, you are good, I am sure," said he glancing at the lace. "Is that thing going to keep you prisoner much longer?"

"No; it is getting done; it will be done in

time," the little girl answered gratefully and happily; and with a smile David left her.

The work went on nicely after that day. Matilda's visions grew glorious, not of Christmas toys, but of changed human life, in one place, at least. She went over and over all sorts of plans and additions to plans; and half unconsciously her lace work grew like her visions, fine and smooth, under her hands. However, Christmas gifts were not to be quite despised or neglected, either; Matilda took time once or twice to go out and make purchases. They were as modest and carefully made purchases as could be. Mrs. Laval she had already provided for, and Norton. For Judy Matilda bought a Scotch book mark or leaf cutter, which cost two shillings. For David, a nice photograph view of Jerusalem. A basket of fruit she sent by express to Poughkeepsie to Maria; and Letitia's dress she matched with a silk cravat for Anne. When these things were off her mind, and out of her purse, Matilda counted carefully the money that was left, and put it away in her trunk with tolerable satisfaction. It was, she thought, a good little fund yet.

Meanwhile the lace-mending was almost done. Mrs. Laval came into Matilda's room on the Thursday morning before Christmas, when Matilda was putting her last touches to the work; and sat for some time watching her. Then suddenly broke out with a new thought, as it seemed.

" You have no dress to wear to-morrow night!"

Matilda looked up in great astonishment.

" Mamma! — there is my red silk — and my green — and my blue crape."

" No white dress. I must have you in white."

" I have a white frock. It is old."

" *That* wouldn't do, you dear child," said Mrs. Laval. " I'll have a muslin for you. Judy will be in white, and so must you."

Matilda bent over her work again with

pulses throbbing and cheeks tingling with pleasure. But in another minute she looked up, and her face had changed.

"How much would that new white dress cost, mamma?"

"I don't know," Mrs. Laval answered carelessly. "Sash and all — twenty or twenty-five dollars perhaps."

Matilda went at her work again, but her fingers trembled. A minute more, and she had thrown it down and was kneeling at Mrs. Laval's knee.

"Mamma, I want to ask you something."

"You may," said Mrs. Laval smiling.

"It is a *great* something."

"I dare say you think so. Well, ask it."

"Mamma, I wish you would let me go without that white dress, and do something else with the money!"

"Something else? What?" said Mrs. Laval, with inward amusement.

In answer to which, Matilda poured out the story of Sarah and her wants, and her

own wishes respecting them. Mrs. Laval
heard her till she had done, and then put
both arms around her and kissed her.

"You dear child!" she said. " You would
like all the world to be saints; wouldn't you ?"

" And so would you, mamma ? "

" I am not one myself," said Mrs. Laval.

"But mamma, you would like all the world
to be comfortable ? "

" Yes, but I cannot reach all the world. I
can reach you."

" This would make me — so very comfortable! mamma."

" But I want you to be as well dressed as
Judy. And I cannot do *everything*."

" Mamma," said Matilda, " I don't care at
all, — in comparison to this."

" I care," said Mrs. Laval. " Is that
dreadful piece of work nearly finished ? "

" Almost, now, mamma." And with a
sigh Matilda sat down to it. She had ventured as far as she thought best. In a few
minutes more the long job was finished.

The shawl was exactly as good as new, Mrs. Laval declared. She made Matilda tell her all about her learning the art of lace-mending; and then broke faith; for she went straight to her mother with the mended shawl and gave her the whole story over again. Matilda did not suspect this; she thought Mrs. Laval had only taken the scarf to put it safely away. Nobody else suspected it, for Mrs. Lloyd gave no token of having become wiser than she was before.

Every thing now centred towards Christmas and the party of Christmas eve. Even Sarah's affairs had to go into the background for the time, though Matilda did not forget them. The Christmas gifts were all ready and safe. An air of mystery and expectation was about all the young people; and a good bustle of preparation occupied the thoughts and the tongues at least of the old. An immense Christmas tree was brought in and planted in a huge green tub in the drawing-room. Mrs. Lloyd and Mrs. Laval and

Mrs. Bartholomew were out a great deal, driving about in the carriage; and bundles and boxes and packages of all shapes came to the house. Matilda and Norton went out Friday morning on some remaining errand of Christmas work; and they found that all the world was more or less in the condition of Mrs. Lloyd's house. Everybody out, everybody busy, everybody happy, more or less; a great quantity of parcels in brown paper travelling about; a universal stir of pleasant intention. Cars and busses went very full, at all times of day, and of all sorts of people; and a certain genial Christmas light was upon the dingy city streets. Only when Matilda passed Sarah Staples at her crossing, or some other child such as she, there came a sort of tightness at her heart; and she felt as if something was wrong even about the holidays.

Cambridge: Press of John Wilson and Son.

www.ingramcontent.com/pod-product-compliance
Lightning Source LLC
Chambersburg PA
CBHW021332110726
47900CB00005B/1441